CHARLOTTE GILL was born in London, England and raised in the United States and Canada. She is a graduate of the MFA program in creative writing at the University of British Columbia. Her work has appeared in many Canadian magazines, *Best Canadian Stories, The Journey Prize Stories,* and has been broadcast on CBC Radio. *Ladykiller* was a finalist for the Governor General's Literary Award. It won the Danuta Gleed Award and the B.C. Book Prize for fiction. Charlotte Gill lives in Vancouver.

Books of Merit

LADYKILLER

LADYKILLER

CHARLOTTE GILL

stories

Thomas Allen Publishers
Toronto

Library and Archives Canada Cataloguing in Publication

Gill, Charlotte, 1971–
Ladykiller : stories / Charlotte Gill.

ISBN 978-0-88762-177-2
I. Title.

PS8613.I435L33 2005   C813'.6   C2005-900059-7

Editor: Patrick Crean
Cover and text design: Gordon Robertson
Cover image: nonstock.com/Veer

Published by Thomas Allen Publishers,
a division of Thomas Allen & Son Limited,
390 Steelcase Road East, Markham ON L3R 1G2

www.thomasallen.ca

 ONTARIO ARTS COUNCIL
CONSEIL DES ARTS DE L'ONTARIO

 Canada Council
for the Arts

The publisher gratefully acknowledges the support of
The Ontario Arts Council for its publishing program.

We acknowledge the support of the Canada Council for the Arts, which
last year invested $20.1 million in writing and publishing throughout Canada.

We acknowledge the Government of Ontario through the
Ontario Media Development Corporation's Ontario Book Initiative.

We acknowledge the financial support of the Government of Canada
through the Canada Book Fund for our publishing activities.

15 14 13 12 11   3 4 5 6 7
Printed and bound in Canada

For my mother

THANKS TO

My family, especially my mother. Kevin Turpin. Zsuzsi Gartner.
Lee Henderson. Nancy Lee. Laisha Rosnau. Chris Tenove.
Jennica Harper. Roland Emery at Bivouac West. Linda Svendsen
and her colleagues in the creative writing department at UBC.
Douglas Glover, Mark Anthony Jarman, and Liz Phillips, who
published some of these stories in earlier forms. The Banff Centre
for the Arts. The Canada Council for the Arts. My agent,
Anne McDermid. Patrick Crean, editor and literary
ninja master, for his faith, patience, and wisdom.

For all the support – bookish, heartfelt,
financial, cosmic – I am endlessly grateful.

PREVIOUSLY PUBLISHED

"The Art of Medicine" in *01: Best Canadian Stories*.
"Hush" in *Grain* and in *The Journey Prize Anthology 15*.
"Ladykiller" appeared as "Mothers" in *The Fiddlehead*.

CONTENTS

YOU DRIVE

What could happen next besides gravity, besides the falling?

The windshield smashed. Glass shattered, grains of glass hung suspended in confused air. Seconds elongated. Their guts compressed as if they were submerging in fluid, a cold miasma of uncertainty. The airbags inflated in great slamming puffs against their chests. They gulped the sudden rush of cold air. Life ripped open, as by a sharp metal hook, and suddenly all things became possible.

The seat belt, the very device that was supposed to save her, ripped at the bowl of her pelvis. She thought she heard his breath amidst all the crushing noise, or perhaps it was her own.

His brand-new truck buckled in all around them, so light for all its heaviness. Metal groaned. Inside the truck plastic twisted and snapped in a spray of snow and ice. The ends of her hair whipped around her mouth. Something hard and sharp struck the back of her head. The truck tumbled with their bodies inside, so slowly and easily that it felt like a cosmic joke. His arm slapped her body as the motion ground down to a shuddering stasis. This was the only sensation that hurt.

After an eternity of jangling motion the truck came to rest right side up, nose-down at a hideous angle. The crumpled hood obscured her view of the slope in front of them. What had stopped their fall? They teetered for several long minutes until it seemed the teetering had always been so.

He heard the clicks and hissing of the ruptured engine. Snow powdered the air. He couldn't turn his head. He made a question of her name.

"I'm okay," she heard herself say as simply as if they were lying next to one another in bed.

Visuals gathered. The airbags deflated in their laps. The front end of the vehicle had compacted like the flimsy metal of a tin can. The dashboard pinioned their legs. She could no longer see their feet, and it made her want to cry. Her face was wet. She touched her own cheek and found blood trickling through her hair from the back of her head. She turned her head to see the steering wheel rammed up against his chest.

She gasped.

"It doesn't hurt." He meant it. He felt etherized, drunk on the absence of pain.

She discovered she could move her arms without much struggle. She touched his parts. Cracked ribs? A punctured lung? She was no doctor. These were the crude diagnostics of an ape-wife, mere guesses at wounds unseen.

He couldn't stop thinking. He huddled away from his body inside the cozy caverns of the mind. In the pit of his belly sat a crystalline feeling, a feathering of cold.

A dull ache spread up from her knees. She shivered into the realization of cold. They lay pinned like fractured insects. The carpet of snow thickened around them without so much as a breath of wind. How long before a passing motorist took note of their lonely tire tracks above, the vanishing hollows in the snow? Small waves of panic cascaded through her body. How long would it take for their rescuers to come? Minutes or hours? They weren't built for this, their soft torsos weren't made to survive this kind of trauma. Was this how one died, without knowing it?

She kept touching him, disrupting the work of his thoughts. Blood screamed through his vessels. Red cells raced like fire trucks to put out his body's fires. But nothing hurt, nothing. His blood was a frenzy of hemoglobin. He had never felt so high.

He was a botanist, of sorts. In his basement he nurtured a plantation. His crops were fed by a complicated array of tubes that dripped perfect ratios of liquid nutrient. Thousands of lumens fed his thriving plants. Timers ran their circadian rhythms. He loved the sappy smell. He loved the constant subterranean summer. He liked to wander between the rows and hear the leaves rustle. The hum of things growing.

Time unfolded as a marathon of seconds. More reality crept in. She caught herself thinking about their blood and how to get it out in the laundry. Look at the mess they were in. She raged with impatience. How long would all of this take?

He laughed out loud. "If we blow up, the whole province will get high." He could hear his ribs creak.

"We're not going to blow up," she said. That only happened in movies.

They feared and hated the police. Their prayers for the arrival of the authorities were new and ironic. They nudged each other from the temptations of unconsciousness. *Are you awake? Don't fall asleep.* They related the storylines of films they'd seen, faking the plot when they couldn't remember. When they ran out of movies, there were the domestic scenarios, the beauty of the life they could have. Someone would have to learn how to cook. They could fill his house with things and more things. She could make feasts and their friends would come by. She could learn how to sew and sell hats at the local fairs. Babies, jars with dried foods in them, explosions of wrapping paper at Christmas. No more lonesome pot pies eaten off the arm of a chair. No more rides from strangers to the far fringes of destiny.

Out of a distant universe came the blessed wail of sirens. They heard them arrive, the rescuers who tumbled down the bank with their headlamps and their radios and their rubber gloves like an army of curious aliens. Now the cops had come to make arrests, to peel them apart.

He asked, "Will you be my wife?"

"You're in shock," she said.

"How do you know?" he said.

She didn't know a single thing. They had gone over the falls like two people in a barrel – perfectly fused with the moment, completely conjoined with each other. Now they drifted in the spume and the mist of the aftermath. Every single second took them farther away. They should have been moaning in agony. They were damaged. They were amazing. Made of soft flesh and yet look how indestructible.

The rear wheels fishtailed here and there and she could see how it pleased him, the tautness, the veering towards and away from danger. His driving terrified her. It made her angry and brave. She twisted in her seat to face him. "Are you trying to kill us both?" she asked, wanting to push it all over from *doing* to *done*.

He jabbed at the stereo's volume button. The interior went quiet except for the engine, the purr of tires on snow.

She wiped a circle of fog off the window and stared out at the winding road. Her thoughts were rotten. She wouldn't say any more.

Around the broad sweep of a curve, the tires slipped a little underneath them. More, then a little too much.

She dug her elbow into the armrest, rising up and back against the seat. From the blur of whitened evergreens, it seemed they were sliding sideways. She looked to him, to the strange orientation of his shoulders, and the sensation was confirmed.

The truck slid out like a secret. It glided obliquely, wider around the bend. He pawed at the wheel, hand over hand as the world outside slurred centrifugally. Of course he would correct this avalanche of motion, negotiate them back from danger to safety. When everything stopped, when their breath returned, she would ask, *What if? Can you imagine?* He was an expert. Nearly everything had happened to him before.

He knew better but braked anyway. The wheels locked. The tires floated over the ice and snow as if treadless. They careened. Sideways, backwards. He turned to her and said plainly, without any trace of panic, as if such events occurred every day of his life: "Hold on."

The rain rolled over them in a spattering torrent. The wipers could barely keep up. They climbed up and up into the next ridge of mountains. The temperature dropped. The road turned slushy with snow.

His truck clipped along through a nondescript channel of forest. In the back of his truck were many pounds of prime-grade hydroponically cultivated marijuana of a strain he himself had derived and gardened to fruition. He had packed it lovingly in garbage bags and Rubbermaid bins. Now he couldn't wait to liquidate it. Now his nose played tricks on him. He could smell money everywhere. He drove hard. He drove to meet a guy named Maurice, who lived in the outer suburban flats of Vancouver. A guy who paid in U.S. cash, who sat far away from tables with a suicidal glint in his eyes.

He drove aggressively. He felt like pushing things to the brink and then bringing them back to safety. The stereo crunched out his music. As a passenger, his last girlfriend never complained. She never got mad. She indulged him in everything. Together they sped, they passed. His last girlfriend bored him to the verge of dementia.

"Could you pull over?" she asked him. "I think I need to pee."

He swerved onto the shoulder. She fell meekly out. In the side mirror he watched her squat in the margin between the shoulder and the ditch, and he thought about driving away.

Snowflakes stung the back of her neck and the fronts of her thighs. She wore a mere patch of skirt. She wondered about her own proclivities, always sexy over sensible.

She came back with snow in her hair. It melted before his eyes.

"What would you do if I left you right here?" he asked.

She looked up and down the highway. Not a single car in sight. She stretched her sleeves down over her hands and let her chin tremble. With men, things went so predictably, cataclysmically wrong. She nudged herself into these endings, as if they were pre-written, and in a peculiar way it satisfied.

He looked out over the steering wheel at the white, wet road. "Get in," he growled.

Why did he bother? Crisis. Complaints. Misery. Maintenance. He had a problem. He ran into women like telephone poles for the pain, the intensity, the continual drama. He knew exactly why. They distracted him from a disease of too much quiet. The sad secrecy of life as a criminal. Which, he reminded himself, was exactly what he was.

She shrunk down in her seat and faced straight ahead. From the folds of her clothing she produced two metal balls and sat them atop the dashboard's smooth gutter. He pointed his eyes at the road. The balls clinked together and rolled apart with each movement of his hand on the wheel. They chimed and clacked, chimed and clacked. On the armrest between them he stretched his fingers wide, then balled them into a fist. Three of his knuckles cracked. He lowered his window and the cab filled with chilly wind. He hurled the metal orbs, first one, then the other, out into the open air.

She drew her knees to her chest and tugged at the roots of her hair. She said, "I am sorry. What makes me do what I do?"

He was relatively clean cut and relatively clean shaven. But look close. Check out the grime under his fingernails. Look at his unwashed hair. Everything about him was dirty, in constant need of laundering. Her dirt was on the inside. She'd like to make them clean with dreams. With lightheartedness. With love.

The truck climbed up over the freezing point. Everything went frigid and drastic and wintry white. The arms of the trees were clotted with snow. The world looked unreal, like the inside of a snow globe.

Clouds roiled and raced. There was no avoiding the bad weather. It was either coming or going, he couldn't tell.

He sat in his truck and waited for what seemed an inappropriately long time. She strode back to the gas bar, with purpose, head down, on the balls of her feet, like a woman in imaginary stilettos. She climbed back into the truck and her body parts arranged themselves into a sly and uncharacteristic quietude. She clicked the tongue of her seat belt into place, and then he was truly suspicious.

A kid in a red shirt – knock kneed, pear shaped – stalked towards them along the same path she had taken. The loaf of fat above his waistband jiggled with every step. The furious pace was a result of something she had done or failed to do. He could tell. He looked at her accusingly. Next he turned the key in the ignition, and the engine purred up. The kid walked the strip of pavement and stopped with his hips aimed at the truck's grille. She kept her attention fixed on the boy, slid her fingers up to the ceiling and through the loop of the handhold.

The clerk approached her window and leaned a forearm against the glass. She looked at the hair and the whitened oblong of skin and thought of a mollusc stuck to the inside of a fish tank. She watched the clerk's eyes dart all over the inside of the truck. They fell on the leather interior and the CDs strewn in the foot well and the stainless steel cup in its holder. The flat of her lap and her flaming cheek. Until she was tired of his gaze all over everything. Tired of his teenaged lust, shot through with contempt. Men found her sexy and freakish and low-life all at one time. Which she was, underneath it all, as well as on the surface.

The boy rapped on the glass with his knuckle. She buzzed her window down an inch and no more.

"What do you want?" she hissed. This, she knew, was the secret to lying. She made big pre-emptive shows of indignation. She made others feel foolish for thinking their thoughts.

The clerk put his mouth to the space above the window. "You stole," he said. He was a lumbering, insecure hick who spoke with a gummy mouth. She was a woman with a keen sense of her own survival. She thought this proudly, and for a second she felt bad for the boy, who might later be whipped for her crimes.

The moment cascaded into a thousand constituent fragments. She shook her head and waggled her finger at the boy. She wondered how life had crept through her, how she crept through life and arrived into right now. The boy's arm fell away from the truck. She turned to her companion and wondered who he was and how she had come to know him. "Drive," she said.

He rammed the truck into gear. He let the clutch out, and the truck rolled. In the rearview the kid's shoulders hung in bewilderment. In the rearview the red shirt shrank and shrank.

He stomped on the gas, and they zoomed past particleboard houses and animals at the end of their chains. Next to him, she arranged herself cross-legged on the seat. She leaned forward towards the windshield and stared out at the road as his dog often did. Sadly, as if rueful about the pavement yet to pass under the tires. They left the town in their wake like they left all unsavoury experience. They tried to shove it in mental receptacles for events not worth remembering.

From her sleeves she produced the things she had stolen. They rested on each of her palms. She gazed at him expectantly, as if they were a gift.

The hairs stood up on the back of his neck. Blood chugged

through his ears. He turned violent corners. The air smelled to him like metal. It charged him up, exposed his nerves, rendered him alive. "Do you have any idea?" he snarled. "Do you think about anything at all?"

There was a dead deer splayed across the pavement. He swerved to avoid the corpse.

"Oh," she gasped, covering her eyes.

Her contradictions astounded him, the hard and the soft. She was the kind of woman who carried spiders out to the grass and pretended elves lived in the cupboard. But she whacked his pet and dangled mice from the pantry by their tails. He thought about love and he thought about lust and how easily the two were confused.

She pulled over on a depressing strip of highway with a Petrocan and a gift shop and a pub with a sign that was lettered in rope.

He opened his eyes, and they fell on her as if she were a stranger.

She shut the truck down and dangled his keys. "I'm done with driving," she said. "You just fall asleep."

He made a squiggle with his finger all around her face. "I wish you'd get rid of that shit." She wore beads in her hair. Glass beads and dreads. "It looks bad," he said. "It makes you look like a pot farmer's girlfriend."

"Am I not?" she asked.

He didn't reply.

He said sexy things and hurtful things, and the trouble was that she lived and died by what fell out of his mouth.

She felt tears jet up out of her ducts, and she whipped herself out of the truck before they could overflow.

Her foot flashed. He saw the upturned edge of her skirt. She left him to pump the gas and pay for it. She hadn't had money since the first day they met.

She crossed the parking lot and took in the sad backwater tableau – the mobile homes and little kids on rollerblades right on the fringes of the highway. She trod through some dying grass towards the gift shop with its screen door and hanging flower baskets and its promise of feminine refuge.

It occurred to her to worry that he'd drive away without her. And if that happened she'd be left without a single cent on her person. She would have to sleep in a room above the tavern until she met some gum-chewing jerk with manure on his boots. Then she'd get married, become a Jehovah's Witness, squeeze out litters of children and by some trick of human adaptation learn to call it happiness. Who would save her from such unfortunate contingencies? She looked back at her man, pumping gas with his eyes hidden behind the reflective lenses of his sunglasses. She needed him more than he needed her, but she was working on ways to make that not quite so true.

She stepped into the store. The clerk was a teenaged boy with zits and hair gooped with gel. He slumped over a magazine with his face against his fist. His eyes travelled up and down her body, stopping at her forehead and again at her feet.

She cruised the aisles of geodes and wind chimes and wooden tulips. Her fingers skimmed a set of Chinese meditation balls, and she picked one up and held it to her ear. The buffed steel, the tumbling inner chimes. She studied her stretched, fish-eyed face on the surface of the ball. The bulbous reflection of the store behind her. The stupid useless wood, the trinkets all around.

She left the shelves and paused in front of the counter. The clerk lifted his cheek from his hand. She ran him clean through with her gaze. She tightened her eyes and kissed the air between them, but it couldn't stop him leering, nor thinking his thoughts. She banged the door open and flew from the store in a funk. A funky, tear-streaked whirl.

A highway patrol car came around the bend. It lurked towards them like a white shark. He fixed his eyes on the headlights. As the two vehicles neared each other he felt his truck sway towards the yellow line as if drawn by the gravity, the pull of self-destruction. He flexed his fingers back against the wheel. The two vehicles passed. In the rearview the cop's tail lights lit up. His pulse leapt up in his throat. His face burned. Then the lights went out and the cruiser sailed around a fringe of trees, continuing on its vigilant way.

After that he said, "You drive. I'm tired."

They stopped to exchange seats. She got in behind the wheel and adjusted the mirrors to suit herself. She did bad, grinding things with the clutch, and this he tolerated in the name of a nap.

She drove like someone who had never owned a car. She veered messily around the fat parts of corners instead of hugging the insides. She drove with both hands on the wheel like a girl who followed the rules. He didn't trust her at all. So he closed his eyes. He folded his arms over his vital organs and pretended to fall asleep.

His body slumped. She looked at him in disgust.

He owned a wonderful house, and she couldn't let herself forget it. It was a tumbledown shack half-wrapped in Tyvek. But inside, the floors were heated, tiled with slate. He lived like a spy, kept his wealth to himself. In the kitchen a stainless steel fridge contained beer and coffee, drinks he consumed in quantity at each end of the day. The biggest, flattest TV she'd ever seen sat in the living room like a time machine. You crossed the room in front of it and let it swallow you up.

The morning air had lost its chill. He pulled off at a rest stop. It was empty. Nevertheless he parked in a clump of trees far from the toilets and the sign-posted map of southern routes. He didn't need to look at any map. He knew exactly where he was.

He led her by the hand over a knoll landscaped with kinnikinnick. He was a botanist, a farmer, and his cargo was his life. Just carrying it around made him feel zingy and endangered. He left the truck unlocked. He felt like acting reckless just to see if the universe was with him.

She carried a rolled-up towel under an arm as if it were a picnic blanket. She threw her shoulders back like she had every right in the world. And there they were, about to spread out the towel and screw in the dappled grass barely out of sight of the highway. They knew one another medium-well, though not through time and vicissitudes.

They were experienced and did an acceptable job pleasing each other. They had easy, separate orgasms. His pants were bunched around his ankles. The back of her skirt was smeared with dandelion pollen. They laughed at the sweet stupidity of their whims and of their mutual need.

They swung their hands all the way back to the truck. Their hands came apart. "We should go to Cuba," she said over the gleaming hood.

"Sure," he said carefully, sliding behind his sunglasses. "Okay."

They climbed back into the truck. She folded her arms and turned away to the window. They had had sex, and now she felt like he owed her something. It was an old-fashioned way to think but it crept up on her anyway.

He turned the key.

"We are the most amazing lovers in the universe," she said.

"Yes," he said. "Indeed."

His valley was a narrow north–south furrow. The sun rose late and set early behind mountains. It burned hotly in the summer, when the hills grew thick with vegetation. But the mountains had been logged many years before, and in winter they still looked bereft.

He looked out the truck windows first at the larch trees and the mountainsides patched with clear-cuts. He was a soft-hearted farmer. He couldn't go anywhere without looking at the way plants grew, without thinking about the angle of the light. They were driving to meet a man named Maurice whom he visited each year, whose address was etched in his mind.

He ate malt balls. He shook them in his fist and threw them into his mouth one at a time. His jaw clenched and unclenched. The sun came out. He put on dark glasses. He felt the deep need to be alone, to crawl inside his brain. He was going to leave her in Vancouver, only she didn't know it yet. She had wacky moods. She didn't believe in reading the newspaper. She'd screw his best friend if he failed to keep her happy, and he wasn't sure he could stomach it.

He settled in for the long drive and prepared for his mood to worsen. He plucked the first of four joints from a Curiously Strong Altoids box on the dash. They drove. Up. They held hands. Over the pass. The air became lighter. They sky grew wide. They smelled dead skunk. They didn't talk at all.

His pot fetish tired her out. She wondered how long it would take him to smoke all four joints and then ask her to roll another. She gazed at the drooping telephone wires and considered just how far they stretched.

Just the sound of the flame, the crackling of cellulose and crystallized resin – it soothed him instantaneously. He skimmed his hand down her bare thigh and whistled. "I love you in that skirt."

And then she was changing her mind. She could be so in love at the drop of a hat, and nothing annoyed her more.

They left the house after omelettes and bacon. They left the plates smeared with grease, the pots piled high with the handles sticking out of the sink. They closed the door on the mess they had made.

They got into his truck. Its slick paint looked like India ink. He slid a disc into the slot of the stereo. The drive nipped it smoothly from his fingers like the soft mouth of a digital bovine. It pleased him. He had been a poor farm boy once.

She sat next to him in her hemp skirt with a paper bag of apple rings on her lap. She felt virtuous and anachronistic and as close to a wife as she ever had.

Only he wasn't her type. For a start, he had a taste for synthetics. He liked music from cold urban plains. He wore expensive shirts made out of polypropylene as if he were a mountaineer or a professional athlete. He was a farmer with a soft belly, but he owned a wonderful house.

He felt racked with the anxiety that he'd left something vital behind. He looked at his house and wondered if he had remembered to do everything. Had he rolled up the hose? Tightened the taps? He wondered if she'd locked the windows as he'd asked. His house stood empty, shut up like a fortress.

They backed down the winding gravel. She played with the idea that she would never return to his beautiful, isolated, enchanted place with the orchard and the unkempt rock gardens and the privacy of the tall grass. None of it was hers, though she thought perhaps one day it might be. She gazed at the roof as if they were embarking on a long and fantastic adventure. The terror was titillating. Life churned like a stomach. Everything turning over.

As they rolled away down the driveway his dog froze, mortally betrayed. Its tail swished between its flanks.

Love. And they weren't even young.

She grew up in Ontario. Her dad was a welder. Her mother cooked meat every single day. Her parents were alive with nothing left to do. They never quarrelled, and they watched too much TV.

His house was the house he grew up in. His last name was Russian because his parents were Doukhobors. They had taught him how to garden and prune fruit trees. But now they were dead.

His town had eight corners and two stoplights. She busked in front of the liquor store. She couldn't quite play and she couldn't quite sing. But she wore a halter top that made him want to ruthlessly scratch an itch. It was no good, this feeling. He looked himself over and saw few things for a woman to like. He threw a red bill down on the purple fur that lined her guitar case.

She winked.

"Come over to my house," he said.

She glanced down at his money. "Later," she teased. "When I'm not so busy."

The house was clean and disused, like it was waiting for somebody. Or mourning someone who'd gone. He didn't cook. Neither could she.

"Stay," he said. And she did.

HUSH

Brian loves Patty in a quiet, sublime sort of a way, always has. He feels lucky, exempt from the marital cycles of jagged passion and boredom. But lately? He hears her shoes on the steps and his ass clenches. Since his *accident*, as he likes to think of it, or perhaps even before, there's been something new. He listens to the long, belaboured pause between the key and the door and her arrival, like nothing in the world is easy. He struggles off the couch, slaps the TV off on the way to the hall, where he greets her with a kiss on the forehead. He makes a feeble play for the grocery bags dangling at her wrists. She wears the trench coat and the Reeboks – a uniform that makes him lose track of the days.

For dinner they are going to have steamed organic spinach with roasted sesame seeds and strands of seaweed that look like little black shoelaces. Patty expresses her mood in some snippy chopping and peeling of vegetables. They are going to eat marinated slabs of tofu, baked on a cookie sheet. Puréed organic parsnips.

At the table he asks, "Is there butter?"

"Butter's full of toxins." She passes him chopsticks. "But you can have applesauce for dessert."

Brian can handle the wacky diet. They have a nice life. They have no children and no plans for children, which is all right since neither one of them can see the point of the constant, low-level chaos. He can handle the tired sighs and the miserable tilt to her eyebrows and the things she almost says but doesn't.

They eat in silence. It passes for appreciation.

After dinner, they do what they always do. She washes, he dries.

"Look," he says. He nudges her with his elbow and points to the window.

Patty's hands leave the sink covered with foam. She steals his dishtowel away.

They huddle at the window together. A snotty evening rain runnels down the glass, obscuring their view of a little round woman trundling up the driveway. She carries a blanketed bundle in one arm, holds her jacket over her head with the other.

"That's the wife," Brian murmurs.

"Look who's been spying." The dishtowel is like a tongue between Patty's folded arms.

"With a baby."

"Uh-oh," she says.

"So far the husband's a putz."

"If we're going to peep," says Patty, "shouldn't we turn off the light?"

Brian watches dating shows back-to-back, the California bozos with capped teeth and the pretty girls with their superior tits. Patty is too pure for all this. But she knits by his side – another Christmas present, another non-surprise he'll try not to wear beyond the driveway. She creeps off her armchair when he's not looking. He notices her absence, slides off the couch and meanders around the house in search.

He finds her hiding behind the bathroom door, already deep into stage one of the complicated oral hygiene regimen that doubles as a means of keeping him – and sex – at bay. By the time she's finished he'll be down on the pillow, turning out the lights in his mind. So he barges in. He watches her spread antibacterial goop on each of her front teeth, then go at the molars with a miniature gumline brush. She looks at him and scrubs harder. Brian plucks the toothbrush from her mouth.

"How are you feeling?" he asks.

"Terrible," she says. Her mouth is full of suds. "But it has nothing to do with you."

When they get into bed, Patty flips from her side to her front, cramming and prodding the pillow underneath her until it's satisfactorily positioned. Brian lies flat on his back.

The doors get locked. The cars in the neighbourhood get parked in their slots. His body winds down. He falls asleep. She falls asleep. The world relaxes. But not tonight. There's something underneath the deep rumble of the furnace and the sigh of their breath. Downstairs the baby is crying. "Oh," Patty groans. She buries her head under the duvet. "Here we go."

The alarm clock goes off like an air horn, slicing through Patty's half-sleep. She drags herself from the blankets, stands on the rug watching Brian, his face collapsed in sleep. For a second she thinks about stuffing his open mouth with the corner of her pillow. She showers and dresses. She feeds herself breakfast and hauls herself down to the car like a great burlap sack of salt with a hole torn in the bottom.

The sky is a big grey pancake with pink light sizzling at its distant edges. She gets into her Honda. She lets it take her to the exit and onto the tapeworm of highway that feeds itself over the bridge. When it comes time to signal and nudge her way into the guts of downtown, she could just keep driving into the mountains. Too bad there's nothing out there but antipodal cravings, nothing in between but deer and rednecks.

The office is deserted. It has the feeling of a surprise party that no one's remembered. She cloisters herself in the corner cubicle where she earns a non-union wage as a tertiary assistant in the tertiary world of HR. On the middle of her desk blotter rests a mussed tower of paper and files. It's hackled with Post-its.

"Go to hell, Wanda," says Patty to the stack.

The phone twitters and she jumps. These days any little thing makes her start. Her hand trembles out to answer it. "Hello?" she says.

"Robin?" It's the man with the creamy, intelligent voice. "Robin Brothers?"

"Didn't you phone me yesterday?" Patty asks.

"No," he says.

"Are you sure? Very, very sure?"

"Totally," he says.

"Well," she sighs. "I'm still not Robin."

"Wrong number," he says and hangs up.

The other girls begin to arrive. *Hello*, they sing to one another. They change their shoes. *Good morning*.

Patty has a recurring daydream of an anonymous man who makes love to her in a nice hotel room with open windows and white curtains while men shout foreign curses in the street below. Who is this man, her nameless, faceless, perfect mate? The weatherman? The man with the intelligent voice? It doesn't matter. She looks for him wherever she goes.

Such thoughts are a horrible waste of time, Patty admits. Perhaps what she needs is a *real* affair. So she can lie like a chromosome, her X to a strange Y on a strange bed with sheets that smell of bleach. So she can wonder who else has screwed furtively or jerked off to porn or perhaps died on the mattress that holds her in its overused trough. Maybe what she needs is something that ends badly.

Patty shoves away from her desk and stands up. Her coworkers sit at their stations, a coven of typing and clicking. Patty stalks down to Wanda's door. She knocks and enters, finds Wanda at her desk surrounded by symmetrical document piles. At her elbow, a giant Starbucks cup with lipstick smeared on the lid.

"I'm not feeling well," says Patty.

Wanda squints at her. "You're kidding. These binders have to go out by three." Wanda is a lean triathlete bitch with smart angular glasses and an angular body that performs like an infallibly well-tuned machine.

"I'm feeling awful," says Patty, "and I'd hate to spread it around."

A week ago, on his rounds, he emptied an ATM in a convenience store. One of the neighbourhood street freaks decided to hook him in the nuts, for no reason at all, with a full bottle of Sprite. Until yesterday he could barely walk. The doctor called it acute contusion and prescribed medication for the pain. But pills do nothing for his pride. They don't stop his Brinks buddies from calling to hassle him. "She gotcha good, didn't she?"

"To tell the truth," Brian says, "I couldn't tell if it was a she or a he."

For now he's laid up at home, dribbling water into the houseplants according to Patty's detailed instructions. The kitchen window looks out onto the back yard, the driveway and the lane, and he watches a gang of guys budge a huge sectional out of a cube van. They'll try to squeak it through the basement door into the suite downstairs. They'll fail, he can see that right now. Someone will come up and knock. Someone who doesn't speak English. They'll want to heave it through Brian's upstairs apartment and go down through the laundry room. Brian will have to agree to watch them ding the drywall and shuffle along on the clean carpet in their dirty boots. Or maybe he'll just say no. The couch belongs to their new downstairs neighbours, who are foreigners.

The former tenant was an old unmarried carpenter from when the neighbourhood was German. He lived off a pension and odd jobs. He didn't smoke or flush at night or run his tools in the house. He didn't have girlfriends. He fixed things that needed fixing. But then he died, and that was the end of a very good thing.

The waiting room is lavishly perfumed with lavender, a scent associated in her mind with her doctor, who wears no lab coat and asks that her patients call her Yasmin. Her inner office is unlike any other doctor's office. There are ferns, fig plants and a wandering Jew. The walls are the colour of sand. There are ambient nature sounds to choose from: Surf, Breeze or Babbling Brook.

"I'm always awake." Patty lies back on the table, which is more like a couch than a table. "Even when I'm asleep."

"I know," says Yasmin, who doctors with a firm, clean hand. "You've said." She begins by probing the arch of Patty's left foot with an electronic pen that reads the state of her insides. Patty stares at the ceiling, nervous about her liver. The machine bleats.

"What does that mean?" Patty wants to know.

"It means you can't tolerate caffeine. Caffeine is full of toxins."

"But I don't drink coffee."

"Then it must be something else."

"What?"

"Don't worry," says Yasmin. "We'll find out."

After the session Yasmin escorts Patty to the waiting room, where she jots things down for the receptionist. She invites the next clients in – a thin, pimply boy and his mother. How vigorous and healthy Yasmin looks by comparison, what perfect skin. Patty wants that skin.

The receptionist fetches two brown dropper bottles from the refrigerator and slides them over the counter along with a sheet of paper, still warm from the printer. Patty's eyes skim over the numbers and columns to the bottom right-hand corner – the total registers like a dizzying height. She presses her hand to her breastbone. "Is this right?" she asks. The receptionist nods and brandishes a pen. Patty takes out her cheques. She signs her wavy name on the straight line and rips the cheque out of the book.

Ever since moving in, the guy downstairs comes out of his apartment between ten and noon with a white plastic grocery bag full of garbage. He dangles it at arm's length by the rabbit-eared handles as if he's not well acquainted with trash. He walks out to the lane and drops it into the garbage can. Then the guy – Brian has learned he goes by Joe (too Anglo, it's suspicious) though they have not yet met – scans up the alley and down the alley from under the duck bill of his ball cap. Then he goes inside.

Today there is no garbage, but two of Joe's buddies roll up in a red Mustang convertible. The driver wears a silver down jacket, though the day is unseasonably warm. The other, a Grizzlies sweatshirt with a hood and cut-off sleeves. Both wear sunglasses and shitty little goatees. They honk the horn and Joe saunters out in Nike shoes worth two hundred bucks, a cell phone pressed to his ear. The guy in the front passenger seat gets out and leaps over the door into the back. Joe gets in next to the driver. The muffler farts out clouds of white smoke. The driver leans forward to retrieve something from the glovebox, obscuring Brian's view of Joe. Then whatever is happening has happened. Joe gets out and heads back to his apartment. The Mustang rumbles away, the muffler like the roll of a big fat snare. Brian writes the licence plate number on the back of his hand.

Drugs, drive-by shootings, B & Es. Brian concerns himself with these things. He has worked in security since he was seventeen. He has worked. He's put in his sweat and his toil. Now he's more than twice seventeen, and his neighbourhood is evolving for the worse. He's not surprised. Entropy is the rule of the cosmos. Events begin well with a few surmountable complications. A taken-for-granted cresting. Then there's the inevitable downhill slide before everything begins to decay. He can think of nothing in life that's exempt from this pattern except for cockroaches and plastic. Nothing important, anyway. Neighbourhoods. Governments, empires, alliances. Buildings and other edifices. Everything goes to shit. Species with no natural predators. Polar ice caps. Bones and teeth and skin. Snowmen. Beauty. Rock bands. Marriage. Love.

Patty walks in. She's early, unexpected. She takes a look at him on the bed and asks, "How's your acute contusion?"

Who puts the cogs back in the universe once all the springs have sprung?

Brian steps down off the bed and lands with a thud on the carpet.

"What else do you get up to when I'm gone?" she wants to know. Patty is a Capricorn, all business about feelings until they're her own. She's still in her coat holding a fistful of keys.

"I keep on top of the highlights," he says darkly.

"What else?"

"Is this a quiz?"

Patty sighs. She brushes her bangs aside, then lets her arm slap down against her handbag. She inserts one of her keys into the niche in the door jamb. She digs around, and sawdust falls to the carpet like dandruff.

"Why are you doing that?" he asks.

She stops. "Did you go down and mention the crying?"

"I went down," he lies. "But there was nobody home."

She pinches her lips to one side. She holds up the end of her scarf, looks at it intently, folds it in half, then in half again.

Patty hustles down the stairs. With each step she charts out what she will say and not say to these neighbours. The baby is not yet crying, but it will, later, when she's in bed, because that's what babies do. Babies need to be wiped and cleaned. They scream and insist. They undo their mothers in public. All that tyrannical, reflexive want packaged up inside something so small and deceptively cute. But it's not the baby she can't stand. It's dependency, helplessness. It's Brian.

She knocks. The door is flung open and Joe appears, looking like a big, neckless bouncer. Patty takes a hesitant step back. "I'm wondering –," she begins, but Joe has disappeared. Patty is left gazing at a pile of big shoes and little shoes on the square of linoleum that separates the laundry room from their neighbours' low-ceilinged zone. Inside the apartment there's a cascade of syllables she can't understand. The smell of onions frying in butter. Where have all these shoes come from? It could be anywhere between Turkey and Bangladesh for all she knows.

Patty hears the swish of legs, nylon against nylon. The wife appears in bare feet, a navy blue Gap T-shirt and warm-up pants. There's a palm-print of flour under the A and the P on her shirt.

She has it all lined up in her mind. She's going to convey her complaint monosyllabically and with gestures. But Patty finds herself forgetting her purpose. She's struck by how young and pretty and round the wife is. She says her own name again and pats herself on the chest.

"Karam," says the wife.

"Karam," Patty repeats. From now on she will want to get it mixed up with *karma*. "Your baby," Patty begins. Despite her intentions, these words leak out sounding accusatory or portentous. Karam's brow furrows. She squares herself in preparation for bad news or complaint. She looks used to bad news and complaints.

It's going to be tougher than Patty thought, this fine line between simplicity and condescension – when you don't speak each other's language, everyone ends up feeling stupider. Patty makes a cradle of her arms. Karam smiles edgily, revealing white, white teeth that have never seen coffee or tea. Before Patty can say more, Karam, too, slips from sight, leaving Patty to wait on the step again.

Karam returns, the nylon rustling softly this time, with the baby in a yellow sleeper. She holds it up for Patty as a testament to its inarguable cuteness. Only the baby isn't pretty.

"Oh," says Patty. She leans in closer. It has a big lolling tongue and pointed lips. Shiny, purplish eyelids. It looks like a little brown turtle with no shell.

Patty had things organized in her mind. She was going to explain that she is a very light sleeper. That she can't do without sleep. That sleep is the most fundamental aspect of good health. But all the fight has drained out of her. "Oh, my," says Patty, touching its sharp fingernails. Fingernails the size of crumbs. Is it sick? Is it deformed? She's forgotten all her lines.

Brian eases bare chested into sheets as crisp and knife edged and as comfortable as parchment.

Patty flips the clasps on her jewellery. "There's something wrong with that baby."

"Well, there's nothing wrong with its lungs."

"It doesn't look *right*." Now she peels off the turtleneck. Underneath it is the familiar beige-toned bra with the wide straps and the mysterious closure.

"Well, what?"

She shrugs.

Brian watches Patty in the final stages of undress. With habitual coyness, she turns away as if she's got a kind of virginity left to keep from him, something not yet seen. She thinks her inner thighs are starting to sag. As if he doesn't already know about her thighs or the pouch of flab around her navel. "Did you mention the thinness of our floors?"

The hem of the nightie flutters down past her shoulders and hips. "I never got that far."

"You lost your nerve."

She flashes on him. "Why are you bugging me?"

"I'm not."

"I had a language barrier to contend with."

"So you point at the baby and cover your ears."

"Why don't *you* point and cover your ears."

This used to be his favourite part of the day. He used to watch Patty shuck off her clothes and her day and think: This woman is my mate. I want to impregnate this person. I want to be worth a million bucks. I want to crawl inside her as if she were a cupboard and taste everything inside.

They stopped sleeping naked after Patty read a book by a doctor from Colorado. According to the book, shoes were a bad idea and bras were a good idea. Sleeping naked was also bad because it disrupted your circadian cycle. For years she'd been turning over, waking herself up with blasts of cold air.

"So sleep closer," Brian said.

When she climbs into bed he fields her like a giant baseball mitt. She fidgets in his embrace. She's used to Brian on night shift, used to sleeping in the middle of the bed. Does she really want to feel the coarse hair on his thigh? Does he really want to feel her cold ass at his hip? Sleeping naked is for other people, couples still fascinated with each other's bodies, for those who can overlook the ingrown stubble and the midnight farts.

She's no fan of the human body, it's true. There are too many ways to get sick. There's a certain type of micro-organism that dwells only on her eyelashes. A zillion kinds of bacteria in her gut. Every day all the earth's fungal spores rain down on her body. Sometimes she hates her own skin. Sometimes she can't scrub hard enough.

"I don't hear anything," she says. "Do you?"

He grunts, disgustingly half-asleep.

"You're too hot," she says, shoving off from him.

She lies awake staring at the darkness, listening to his breath descend into the deep, familiar rasps of a snore. No one ever died because of lack of sleep? She's read experiments on sleep deprivation in rats. After three days with no sleep they claw and tear at each other's fur. After a week they burrow into their corners and lie there inert.

A few streets away, a siren Dopplers by and her whole body tenses. It's not the crying baby itself but the *idea* of a crying baby, the proximity of stress and discomfort, the *waiting* that shreds the quiet in her mind. Brian sleeps, oblivious. The siren sets the rotten dog howling behind the fence next door. Patty holds her breath. When the crying begins, it's no surprise. It travels up from the basement, up the stairwell and through the rooms of their apartment and into her ear canals. The wailing begins light and faint, then blossoms into waves of shrieking and gasping. Her mind follows the cadence, a lump of anger rising up in her throat. She pounces up on all fours. Brian turns onto his side and reaches for her shoulder.

"Don't." She quivers on the verge of tears. "Don't even touch me."

The horizon pukes sherbety light on another gorgeous morning. Patty storms out of bed, throws her clothes on the bed and stomps around on her heels over every square foot of the apartment. She feels like a stretched length of yarn, like something dangled from a rooftop. Brian appears, puffy eyed. His big goofy hands scratch around in the pockets of his robe.

"What's up?" he asks.

"I'm going to *work*." She looks at him through eye slits, on the verge of some dangerous honesty. She fumes into the hall and snatches her coat off its hook. Brian's slippers scuff along the floor. *Pick up your goddamn feet*, she thinks.

"Look," says Brian at the door to the basement, which is ajar. On the floor between the door and the jamb rests a palm-sized lump, wrapped in coloured cellophane. He nudges it with his toe, then picks it up. "This must be for you."

"How do you know?"

"It's pink, for a start."

She takes it out of his hands and yanks at the corkscrew of ribbon. The plastic comes apart. Inside are four white cakes, cut into the shapes of diamonds. She holds one to her nose and the smell is nearly indescribable, like rose petals, crushed and wet, but also something creamy and edible. It reminds her of something she can't quite place. Something lovely. From childhood.

"Is that soap?" Brian asks. "It looks like soap."

She peeks through the open door into the unlit stairwell and catches a whiff of another smell that isn't hers or Brian's, a smell that's decisively *theirs*. Without thinking, Patty lifts one to her mouth and nibbles a corner. A milky sweetness floods over her tongue. Her eyes water – she hasn't had sugar in years. "It's not soap," she says. Though she'd rather it was.

Brian wanders from room to room, forgetting his purpose. Perhaps all that's needed is a little air, some locomotion. He pokes his head through the neck hole of the Harvard sweatshirt – a gift from his mother, who trots off to all parts since the death of his father – as yet unworn. He slides his arms into it but then takes it off because only morons advertise the fact of their non-education. He's very happy and mostly optimistic, but the world has its lucent truths.

The weather's fine. Sun-dappled sidewalks, a moist breeze. He begins at a careful stroll, assessing the status of his injury. All is fine. The rhododendrons bloom. The aroma of flowers is everywhere.

He proceeds to the park without deciding to. At the gates an old guy hurries a Yorkie down the asphalt path. "Come on, Rippy." Rippy sniffs and pees on the underbrush. "Rippy, let's go." The guy becomes resentful, yanks Rippy along in his harness. It's his wife's dog, obviously.

Brian quickens his pace to a vigourous walk. But three-quarters of the way around the path a knifing pain shoots through what he's sure must be his prostate.

He hobbles around the circuit in the requisite direction,

perturbed by the pedestrian traffic. Suddenly everyone's annoying. The skateboard punks, the old dames, slow as ducks. *Get a job*, he wants to say to everyone he passes. Even the chatty girls with the high ponytails and the nice calves and the pompoms at the heels of their socks.

Brian limps back to the house. He finds Patty, back again early from work, cross-legged on the couch, staring at the sky beyond the window. No guy likes to see his wife in a meltdown – after all, it's probably his fault – but this is terrible. Patty's face leaks tears and mucus. His nuts throb with a vicious ache. He thinks of this pain as laden with meaning, there to punish or humble him in some medicinal, necessary way. Her hand clutches out at his, her fingers chilled and moist.

"Can't you hear it?" she asks.

The next thought that darts through his mind startles him: *What if she's gone crazy?* "I don't hear a thing." He crafts the sentence with his least inoffensive tone.

"Smell that," she says. "Do you smell that?" Patty has burst into the room where Brian wipes polish onto his work boots in slow, deliberate strokes.

He sniffs and shrugs.

"It's electrical." Her nose works the air like a marsupial's. "Like hot metal." Her eyes land on the blackened rag between his fingers, the boot between his knees. She gasps and rolls her eyes as if he's the most obtuse human being she's ever known. She whirls and flees the scene.

"That hurts," he says to the wall.

When the smoke detector starts to blare downstairs, she collides with him in the hallway. "Fire," she says, clutching him by the buttons and the chest hair. "They're trying to burn the house down." He disentangles her fingers but lets her drag him by the forearm down the basement steps to the laundry, where their downstairs neighbours have spread out an assortment of belongings. Brian and Patty walk the narrow path of clean floor past the washing machine. Patty nudges things out of the way with the side of her foot and the back of her hand – satin blankets and underwear strung on clotheslines and garbage bags full of extra whatever.

Patty pounds on the door. Brian can see her thinking what she's already told him dozens of times: These are people who never throw things out. Who will never teach their child not to shriek for attention. Who believe in nylon and polyester and disposable diapers. Who sweep the floor but not the corners. They're those kind of people.

The door opens. The smoke detector blasts out at them like an auditory wind – a noise so loud all of Brian's body hair stands up. Joe emerges in a black Gold's Gym T-shirt, yacking urgently into a cordless phone over the sound.

Brian sees they are exactly the same height. He can look Joe straight in the eye.

"Where is the fire?" Patty demands. The urgent authority in her voice makes Joe step aside in the door. Patty attempts to dart past him into the house, but he stops her by the forearm and points down at her feet. "Oh, give me a break," says Patty, kicking off her shoes in an exasperated rush.

In his socks Brian steps into the apartment, which is different from what he remembers. Long tubes of fluorescent light and commercial-grade low-pile carpet, stone grey, the same as in the office where his supervisor and the dispatch girls work. Good for high traffic, stain resistance, rug burns.

A stratum of thin blue smoke hovers a foot from the ceiling. Patty zips instinctively into the kitchen. Brian follows her. Joe follows Brian. Patty scans the stove dials and pulls at the oven door. It won't open.

"What's in here?" she yells at Joe. Joe shrugs. He's off the phone now but holds it in his hand. "What do you mean you don't know? Where the hell is your wife?" He pulls at his lower lip, guilty and bewildered. She points to a knob. "Do you know what you did? You put your pizza on self-clean. The door won't open until the cycle's done." She touches the stove with her finger, then withdraws it quickly. She makes a sizzling sound with her mouth.

Patty is formidable. "I think he understands the *hot* part," Brian says. Brian almost feels bad for Joe.

Next Patty bustles to the smoke detector, which she's too short to reach. "Kill it," she shouts with her eyes closed, fingers in her ears.

Brian comes to her aid, reaches to the ceiling and rips the cover off. He pulls the wire cap from the nine-volt and they are plunged into sudden quiet. Joe peers over their shoulders like a passerby. Brian glances at the leaping white cat and the bolt of lightning on the battery's casing, then hands it to Joe. Joe stares at it on the flat of his palm.

Patty points at the stove. "Move it for me, Moose," she commands.

"What if I get electrocuted?" asks Brian. She hasn't called him Moose in ten years.

Patty sets her hand on the oven door's handle. "We'll get electrocuted together."

Joe slides into his wife's oven mitts. Brian wraps two dishtowels around his hands. He touches the corner of the stove and breaks into an instant sweat. He and Joe grunt and jiggle and scrape the thing away from the wall.

When there's room Patty dives in behind it, wiggles her slight frame into the space they've made for her. Brian peeks over the back where Patty, bent sideways at the waist, works the plug prongs back and forth. She stands up. "There." She drops the cord on the floor like a snake she's just strangled with her bare hands.

Brian and Joe stand there looking at each other as if they should shake hands. Patty cocks her ear towards deeper regions of the apartment, then moves off down the narrow strip of hallway. Brian and Joe follow.

At the end of the hallway are two closed doors. Patty turns the knob on one of these, and the baby's cries blare out at them from the darkness. Patty steps into it. Brian dips his head into the room, allowing his eyes to adjust. Patty makes shushing noises on her way to the crib, which isn't a crib at all but a small mattress on the floor with cushions wedged under the edges.

Halfway across the room, Patty gasps. Brian sees her silhouette jump. He pushes the door open wider and the light falls upon the glossy eyes of Karam, who sits cross-legged in the middle of this mattress, in the dark, rocking with the baby in her arms. As if she could escape from the noise and the smoke by playing hide-and-go-seek. Patty shoots Brian an over-the-shoulder look. *What are these people thinking?*

Upstairs Patty flings open all the windows. Brian trails after her like a simpering boob from room to room so that she can't think straight. "That baby's going to cry until the end of time," she laments.

"It won't."

"We're going to go mad."

"We'll move."

"No way," she says, stomping her foot for emphasis. "We were here first."

"Well, we'll make sure and tell them that."

"You're no help at all."

He looks at her and sighs. "What do you want me to say? That the baby is crying on purpose just to piss you off?"

Patty throws her arms up in the air. They are back in the kitchen where they started. How should she know why babies cry? She doesn't have one. She and Brian are DINKs with the combined income of a veteran Safeway cashier. But why stop there? Here's to not going on vacations. Here's to renting, not buying. To their postal code. The White Spot. Rusty shitbox cars. Here's to Winners and Payless. No frills and bag lunches. Here's to no kids. To having run out of ways to amuse oneself.

Patty slings her purse onto the counter by the straps. She rifles through to the very bottom in search of her wallet.

Brian hovers at her side with the meat of his palm on the sink's edge.

"How much cash have you got?" she asks.

He slides his wallet out of his back pocket and counts out a few well-used, flannel-textured bills. "What for?" he asks. "Are you planning to *buy* the baby?"

She nips at his money with the ends of her fingers. Brian holds it in the air just beyond her reach.

"Give it to me," says Patty.

"No," says Brian.

"Fine then." She clicks her wallet shut and hurls it back in her purse.

"Things will change," says Brian. "Babies grow up."

A little muscle under her left eye twitches and flutters. "Not always," she sneers. "Look at you."

Yes, look at men: Husbands get sympathetically sick the very minute their wives come down with the flu. They don't clean toilets. They can only handle one thing at a time. They punch out at five. Nothing's their fault. They'd rather be golfing. They are dogs in the institution of marriage. Lumbering, dumb. Always getting tangled up in your legs.

"Why do you do that?" Brian complains.

"What?"

"*That.* Half a fight, and you're not happy until it's a whole one."

"Because you push me to it."

"What have I done?"

"Exactly. What have you done? It takes you three months just to get up in the morning." She watches his expression to see what will happen to it. It wavers. A shiver of satisfaction creeps over her scalp. Brian holds his index finger aloft and begins to say something, then gives the air between them a broad sweep with the back of his hand. He stomps out. Patty leans against the cutlery drawer. Downstairs the baby is still crying. She can't feel sorry. She hasn't slept. It's all the baby's fault.

Patty charges downstairs yet again. She knocks on the door. When Joe answers, the light behind his head is dazzling. She steps up to him. "Look at these," she says. She shows him the aggravated pinks of her underlids. "You on the other hand have no wrinkles and the whites of your eyes are still white and I think you could sleep through a nuclear attack and still have good dreams." She begins to work the money in her hand into a tight little tube. "Who gets up at night and feeds that baby? I bet two hundred bucks it isn't you." She prods it into the dorky, ornamental pocket halfway up Joe's sleeve. He backs away, startled by the alien feminine touch, so that she has to lean in to complete the delivery. "Understand?" she asks, stepping down her tone a notch, trying not to sound like a small-minded bitch. "Yes?" She nods. "No?" She shakes her head.

Joe shoots her a strange sidelong glance. Perhaps he has no idea what she's saying. But then no one's that stupid when money's around. "That's a gift," she says, pointing to his pocket. "Take the baby to a nice hotel for a night. Or two. Give your poor wife a break."

Patty shuts the door and leans against the wall. Brian measures out tea leaves from one of her little plastic bags not because he likes the taste but because something has come in with her, like a front of black weather. Something that needs a placebo, some calming, some combing down.

Patty rubs her finger back and forth over her thumbnail. She starts to cry. He drops the tea ball into the pot and the chain goes slithering in after it. He walks over to her and takes her hands in his big fists. He kisses the ends of her fingers. He kisses her wet face.

"I hate everything," she says.

"No, you don't," he tells her. She pulls her hands away and presses her fingertips into her eye sockets. The kettle starts to rumble. He collects her in his arms like a tightly bound bundle of something, newspapers or laundry.

She can't see the light in anything. She finds nothing funny. She never did. He wants to feed her a bloody steak in small bites. He wants to lay her out under a tropical sun. He wants to carry her into the bedroom and peel the clothes away. He feels like covering his wife and injecting her with happiness. If only it were transferable, like cash or body heat, this thing that he has that she doesn't. The average contentment she jealously despises, that makes her hate him along with the rest of the world.

Brian arrives in the locker room with his uniform already on and his duffel in hand. He finds the night-shift guys, his old pals, changing from their uniforms into sweatpants and down vests and white sneakers. His supervisor has slotted Brian into daytime detail, a lucky switch, though one made with no explanation. He tries not to think it's because of his new testicular vulnerability.

His locker is marked with his name. He looks at the label, the way in which he formed the letters of his own name so long ago. He opens his locker, and the door falls open with a clang. He drops his bag into the bottom, and when he turns, his buddies have stopped lacing up shoes and fastening Velcro to look at him.

"Hey guys," Brian says tentatively.

"How's it hanging?" they tease, but they've missed him. They slap him on the back and they high-five. They say, "Hey, man, good to have you back."

But something's changed or missing or maybe he's just being paranoid. Minutes later they are trickling out of the locker room in a gaggle. He's left there, the first guy to show up for the changing of the guard. Brian sits down on the bench with his jacket on until the day shift arrives, one by one. They mill and unzip. They open and close lockers. How long will it take for them to notice him?

Patty dealt with the neighbours. No more crying. There is so little movement downstairs, Brian begins to forget they all share the house. No longer does he shift limb by limb into bed, apologizing as if Patty has caught him watching porn or kicking the pet they don't have.

They lie on their pillows. "Isn't this nice?" asks Brian.

"Shhh," says Patty. "You'll hex it."

Sleep, after not sleeping, is the most delicious pleasure known to man. They tumble into it and doze through the alarm in the morning. They wake up to the radio show banter of Larry and Willy. They are getting to like it.

It's raining after days with no rain. Pigeons are cooing under the eaves. Patty lifts the elastic of his pyjamas. Her light hand settles on his cock and waits there like a thrilling, electric question he's afraid to answer. There's his handicap down there – what if he's lost his aim? But mostly it's been a very long, delicate time between them.

"Does this hurt?" she asks. Her hands probe around. "Does this?"

"You're going to make me late."

"Just answer the question."

"No," he says, "it doesn't hurt at all."

In Yasmin's waiting room, Patty reads a yoga magazine, flipping pages without registering the content. Yasmin comes out to fetch her. Yasmin, with hair drawn back in a slick dark coil, a severe part on the side. She smiles a flat little smile. Patty wonders if she's done something wrong, or if it's just Yasmin's mood. Did someone piss her off? Patty wonders what Yasmin's house looks like and who shares it with her. She wonders if Yasmin is a lesbian.

Patty follows Yasmin into her office and they begin the procedure. "Lie down," says Yasmin, though Patty knows exactly what to do – this Thursday as with every Thursday. Yasmin goes to the head of the table and leans over Patty, rubbing her palms together. She plunges her thumbs and fingers into Patty's hair.

Patty tells Yasmin what's gone wrong with her body during the week. Yasmin listens and massages little circles into Patty's scalp. Patty relates the intricacies of her dietary regimens. Yasmin listens and hums. The humming annoys Patty. She begins to embellish the story of her body, while reclined on the vinyl, just to see if Yasmin is listening. "I had an all-over rash," Patty says. "I've been experiencing nausea." But Patty has been feeling like an ox, like the healthiest ox on earth.

"Are you hydrated?" Yasmin asks. "Maybe you need a new water filter. Have you thought about buying distilled?"

Has Yasmin thought about varying her pattern? This is getting tired. Each week Patty talks. Yasmin listens, sort of. She praises Patty for her diligence with diet or the purity of her constitution. But praise is just the beginning. Here's what else Patty must try. Patty must purchase this or that product, or improve her self-discipline. Patty must climb higher for Yasmin. Nothing's good enough, or else Patty would not be here, she'd be cured. *Cured* – as with disease, as with leather – the word lingers in Patty's thoughts until she begins to doubt its meaning.

Yasmin works the base of Patty's skull. "You're loose back there," says Yasmin. "That's good. Most people are very tight."

But Patty doesn't want to be loose or easy. She'd rather be hard, a puzzle for someone to solve. She opens her eyes and peers up at Yasmin. Yasmin stops kneading. She smiles. Upside-down it looks as if she's baring her teeth.

Brian arrives home from work to the aroma of basted meat. He salivates wildly. "What's on?" he says, clutching Patty by the hips.

"Free-range lemon chicken. Roasted tarragon potatoes."

He could kiss the ground, they're eating *food* again, but he doesn't want to discourage her with too much enthusiasm. "I could eat my left arm." He bends to her lips, then straightens. "Oh," he says. "You cut your hair." He runs his fingers through a few stubby strands of it.

"Do you like it?" she asks.

"I like it," he says wistfully. "I love it."

When they sit down at the table, Brian devours half his meal without taking his eyes off the plate. Patty falls quiet, knifing little slivers from her vegetables. He's picking chicken flesh from a bone by the time he notices.

"What's wrong?" he asks. "Not hungry?" She sets down her knife and her fork on the edge of her plate. She shakes her head. He wonders if she's going to cry.

The phone rings. Patty rushes for it.

"Leave it," he says. She sinks back down and dabs at her mouth with her napkin, which she then shoves under the table onto her lap.

The answering machine in the hall whirs and beeps. They listen to a glottal voice. It sounds like no one they know. Somebody overweight. Somebody pissed off.

"This is Gus. Remember me? I used to work the day shift. Well listen, pal, I hope you're satisfied. Because now I'm stuck with your shitty night-shift leftovers. What were you thinking, you stupid jerk? You and your busted ball."

Now it's her idea to make love in the middle of the night, though furtively, with the lights out, once she's assured herself that everyone else is asleep. She wants to make up for something. She wants to knock herself out. Brian is going to let her.

He is going to lie on top of her and try to be light. He is going to try not to think of his busted ball. He's going to try and be a good lover. To look down at her and see her as beautiful. He is going to try to be *present* as she's asked – whatever that means. But there's something that keeps distracting him. They are not what they used to be.

Downstairs, there is the click of a light switch. It's the start of something. Trouble, or rather, a restlessness. They hear Karam's voice, then Joe's. Lately they've been hearing a lot of midnight conversation: There is an exchange of information. Sometimes the conversation ends in a verbal skirmish and sometimes it just ends. Then there's the aftermath, the flushing of the toilet, the whoosh of water in the pipes. The TV.

Patty whispers, "Stop."

He does, still inside her. He waits. Then thrusts himself deeper as if she won't notice.

"Don't," she says testily. She turns her head on the pillow, straining towards the muffled volley of words. "Now I can't." She slides out from under him, drapes her arm across her forehead as if to cover a fever or a migraine.

"You don't really want to do this, do you?" says Brian.

She closes her eyes and winces. "I spent four thousand dollars at the naturopath."

He props himself up on an elbow. "Say that again."

"Things got a little carried away."

"What things?"

"We're overdrawn." She pummels the pillow and throws herself down on it with a dissatisfied groan. "The Master-Card is maxed."

Brian gapes at the back of her head, his body tingling, his penis at attention.

Cars glide up and down the alley with music streaming from the windows. Kids tear by with balls and sticks and roller-blades. An evening on the cusp of summer. The whole neigh-bourhood is out in the balm of it.

Brian sips from a wine glass. Patty sits on a lawn chair, arms folded, one knob of bony knee slung over the other. He sets the glass down on the barbecue's wooden slats. He prods and flips things on the grill. Fat drips and flares. When Patty thinks he's not looking, she picks up his glass. He sees her from the corner of his eye. She tips the glass back and a quar-ter of its contents disappear into her mouth. She puts the glass back, sluices the mouthful around, swallows. It's an evening on the cusp of everything.

Downstairs there is the opening of a door followed by the bang of the knob against the wall. Patty swivels towards the noise. Brian leans out over the railing. Karam comes into view in an ankle-length bathrobe. She's barefoot. Her hair is undone from its usual tight braid. It fans out down her back, in bobbing, unbrushed waves.

Brian and Patty watch her travel down the driveway.

Towards the bottom she steps on something sharp, a piece of gravel or a cube of tempered glass. She lets out a startled yelp and continues into the lane at a limping half-jog. They watch her pink soles recede in the dusk. As she slips from view behind a garage, they glimpse the hem of her robe, the trailing end of her long skein of hair.

Brian raises his eyebrows at Patty.

"Don't look at me," she says.

Karam reappears on the other side of the garage having picked up some flapping, uncontrolled speed on the laneway's decline. She runs not to fetch something but *away* from something. Like a cloud of bees or a tormenting itch. Or out of her own skin. Then she's gone. Slipped out of view behind a cedar hedge.

Joe emerges, walks his measured, stooped walk to the end of the driveway. He stops in the alley, looks right and then left. He glances back at the house and catches sight of Brian and Patty on their balcony. He flashes them a distracted, phony, wobbling smile. Patty lifts her arm into a column of charcoal smoke as if to wave or to beckon. She points after his wife, down to the right, towards the park. Joe doesn't nod or acknowledge the signal. He takes off with his head down. He doesn't call her name. No one calls her name.

"Should we help or something?"

"Like what did you have in mind?" asks Brian. Call the cops? Phone an ambulance? Weird, private things go on between couples.

Patty steps inside to the kitchen and comes back out with a glass of her own, which she presents to Brian, an empty vessel to be filled. He peers right into the black hole of her pupil while slopping Chardonnay into her glass. They exchange a conversation of looks:

Drinking?

Don't hassle me.

It's been a long time.

I don't care.

Brian holds the tongs aloft. He wears Patty's apron with the geese on it and an oven mitt with geese on it, and suddenly he feels like an ass, like a pussywhipped jerk. Patty is his wife, his closest companion. But right now he'd like to toss his wine in her face, gun her down with an icy spray from the garden hose. What kind of love is this?

A drawer rolls open, and it's a clue. The contents scuttle and collide with the front of the drawer, and someone – Joe, Brian guesses from the roughness of manner – roots around in search of the necessary item. Downstairs, they sleep in the day and stay up all night, their routine flipped like cushions in a ransacked house. Brian hears Joe snoring when he comes home from work. Downstairs, they save their common, everyday sounds for the middle of the night: The tapping of toothbrushes against the porcelain in the sink. The stacking of plates in the dish rack. Patty pounces up out of sleep.

Where is the baby? Brian and Patty aren't sure, but they have unmentionable ideas. They skulk about in separate bubbles of solitude. It feels like a kind of embarrassment.

Brian sits down to loosen his laces in the kitchen, making a study of the shoe itself. The grommets, the lace tips, the side-slipped tongue. There's the tick of the clock in the kitchen and the burbling of the drain upstairs. When the shower stops he thinks he can hear Patty drying herself. After a while he lumbers up the stairs, one foot then the next.

He finds her perched on a corner of the bed. Slippers on her feet, legs crossed, hair turbaned in a towel. She pinches the bathrobe closed at her clavicle, rubs the terry between thumb and forefinger. She has lavender puffs under her eyes. There is a plate on the bed. She begins slicing a pear into four. All Brian can see is juice dripping off the blade of her knife. She wraps the pear wedge in prosciutto. She pushes it into her mouth.

"Where the hell did you get that ham?" Brian demands. "How much did it cost?"

What are babies but a fraction of an adult? It was one-tenth the size of Patty. One-tenth of her weight and adult proportions. An unformed personality. A sickly, soft-boned, toothless creature. Perhaps a tenth is too much. How about half of a tenth? A twentieth. A fraction of a fraction.

Do they go down? Do they ask? How will they know for sure?

Babies are the commonest, easiest thing to make. Every-where, all over the world, people wind up with little repro-ductions of themselves. Mothers jerk them around in the bath trying to lather soap onto all the right body parts, trying to wash the dirt of life from their faces and armpits. They shake the poop out of diapers. But it's no use. You can't make life fair just by getting it clean.

Anxiety sits like a brown clayey lump in the middle of her mind. Patty can't push it around. Why worry? It's a useless emotion. It's not real. It can't touch her. She decides to march forth in her thoughts. The car is nice. She is going to be happy and positive. She's going to sit in deep traffic, listening to a dreamy male voice on the radio. She's going to imagine what this man looks like, and if he would find her sexy.

Then, while she's stopped at the intersection, there's an ambulance. Its lights flash in her rearview. There are too many cars. It's a tight situation. She's stopped too close to the minivan in front of her. She honks at the driver to move up. He glances at her in his mirror and then back to the car in front of him. Behind her, the streams of traffic are parting. The ambulance is upon her, its sirens insisting in their professional way that she move, move, move. She cranks the wheel and clenches her teeth, breathing, breathing deeply all the time. The car is her enclave of warmth and protection. She wedges it out of her lane between the minivan and a pickup parked at the curb. The ambulance squeaks by her door, a big white box. As it passes the paramedic in the passenger seat shoots her a nasty look. The paramedic with his fleece vest and his short, white sleeves. Why? It's not her fault she's involved. Nothing is her fault.

The ambulance speeds away, but somehow not fast enough. What about the person on the gurney in the back? Is she dying? Is someone holding her hand? The mere thought of it makes the tears crest on the rims of her eyelids. But now she's waited too long to get back into the flow on the street. Now she's waiting some more, nosing into the stream of cars whose owners pretend not to see her. Her neck hurts from craning. She butts back in. A car honks and she's clouded in a sudden fog of emotion. When the time comes, who will want to hold Patty's hand? Her life is too small, her desires too selfish and nasty. Who will sit by her hospital bed while tubes pump fluids to replenish what has leaked? She feels as if she's leaking right now. Who will applaud when she triumphs over death? She's back in the thick of the rush-hour tide. She lets it carry her home. She turns her corner. It's too close to home to cry.

Three women stand in the driveway, two young, one old. They have noses exactly like every woman Patty has ever seen enter the downstairs apartment. They stare. Patty smiles. They don't. As she climbs the steps, Patty feels their eyes on the triangle of scarf across her back, her stockinged calves where the muscles begin to burn. She has the key ready in her hand. She scurries inside and closes the door and leans her full weight against it.

Brian slouches in to greet her. He's so slow and dour. He's got something to tell her, she can tell. It's going to be creepy and bad. The light fades in the house. Brian approaches. He tries to wrap his hand around hers. She slaps him away. He wants to slather her with sympathy. He wants to drool all over her parade. Cars and more purring cars in the driveway. Doors thud softly. Clouds slide over the sun – her least favourite weather of all, when you want to turn the lights on before it's even dark. Their apartment is too white. They never entertain. They need to cover the walls. Polite little heels click across the asphalt. Downstairs the apartment fills with murmuring women. What's the matter with these people downstairs? They're not normal. Why don't they shout and kick holes in the walls? Why don't they scream at the ceiling and be done with it? Go fuck yourselves, she'd love to yell out over the rooftops. She doesn't want their news. They can keep their goddamn news to themselves. She's going to call up some people and invite them for dinner. She's worked hard for this mood. This unbearably fantastic mood.

LADYKILLER

They embark in Roz's car, a practical sedan of foreign make from a design phase when cars were built to look like cigarette packaging, streamlined and boxy at the same time. It's raining, yet even more wintry inside the car. Gary drives. They don't talk. They don't even listen to music. They sit in their silence as psychic snow drifts up against the windows. Roz looks straight ahead, cracking her ankle every few minutes, then slapping her glove like a leather tongue against her lap. The highway passes underneath them, slick and black. Water shushes in the tire wells.

Three days before Christmas, the next-to-shortest day of the year. Holiday traffic is backed up a million miles from the ferry terminal. Roz insisted they leave at this hour. Gary had wanted to sleep late. Now she looks straight ahead with her legs crossed and her hands intermeshed. A satisfied frown at the corners of her mouth like, who was he to doubt her? Workers with flashlights and high-viz vests direct traffic onto the shoulder of the highway. They permit a strip of this millipede to crawl off the boats. The sky goes a fecund shade of eggplant. Clouds, the possible sun.

Roz wants to go up to the top decks. She gives him a sort of kiss-off with her middle and index fingers.

Gary stays behind in the car with a newspaper spread over the wheel. Roz has left him alone and a thin film of worry coats all of his thoughts. In his chest, the press of amorphous dread. He runs his eyes over chunks of text, his mind absorbing nothing. They are on their way to his mother's, Gary's boyhood home. The visit looms. A boredom verging on anxiety. It drives him out from seclusion onto the vehicle deck in search of some visual distraction.

The ferry's hold is like the gut of a giant mechanical behemoth. The walls and the floor are grimed over with grey-brown soot. Cars and trucks packed bumper to bumper, lit by caged fluorescent tubes. He prowls the rows. Underneath him the boat engines rumble.

Few passengers remain down below. Poodles left behind, yapping at inched-down windows. His eye is drawn to the interior of a sedan where a girl dozes on a reclined seat with her back to the door. Headphones, a rectangle of exposed skin, low-riding pants, coloured thong floss peeping over the waistband. Gary collects the visuals, then veers towards the ferry's outer edges where a stiff sea wind pours in.

There he catches sight of a sheet of billowing hair, a woman leaning out over the railing. Blonde, from a bottle, he can tell from its flat lustre. She wears a cropped silver parka of the variety worn by cheerleaders – an amenable sign. He surveys the curves and contours of her lower half, and finding himself pleased, tucks into the narrow strip between the cars and the railing to further his investigations. She has her elbow propped on the railing and her chin in her hand, and she looks out at the sea, he thinks, wistfully. She ignores his approach. It only serves to encourage him. His stride grows energetic, his shoulders lift – with each step closer he's starting something. A motion, like a sneeze, that can't be stopped once triggered.

Gary swoops and dives. He takes his hands out of his pockets, and as he squeezes past her, grazes his knuckles across her sacrum. He skims his nose through her hair, which smells of vanilla and showered wetness. Sensations penetrate like X-rays, his bones lit up with strange touch. Then the contact breaks and the world flattens out again. He sweeps and passes through.

Gary continues on, waiting until he's put the lengths of a dozen cars between them before giving her an over-the-shoulder glance. She's looking straight at him with an expression he's seen many times before – halfway between amusement and outrage. He quickens his pace and disappears around the bulkhead before he invites more trouble than can be refused.

The stock rooms, the service elevators, the fire stairs, the airport bathrooms, the least frequented wings of public places, the unvisited hallways of the mind. On some occasions there's more, sometimes just this – an unknown female, whiffs of hope and relief, a feeling of continuous arrival.

Gary travels back to the car, enjoying the soft pause in his thoughts. Across the water is their island destination, cloaked in rain shadow. He looks out at the horizon where the sky turns pink, and he remembers what it's like to be free.

The ferry nudges up against land and disgorges their car. Gary relinquishes the driving to Roz. The traffic around the terminal is heinous and claustrophobic, the streets rampant with roadside convenience. Wal-Mart, Canadian Tire, Overwaitea Foods. Everyone shopping, eating fast food, driving, parking, making mountains of garbage. Home – he could rip off his shirt, run screaming into the ocean and begin the swim back to the mainland.

As soon as the tires hit the highway, Gary says, "Let me out."

"What?"

"I can't go," he says. "Let me out. On the corner will be fine." He points at the curb where a guy battles the weather in a clown suit, between the planks of a sandwich board advertising roses.

Roz swerves over onto the shoulder and squeaks to a halt. Gary reaches for the door. But before he can make his escape Roz has her finger on the button. All four door locks ratchet down. They sit there for a time with the engine idling, the muffler puffing smoke. He can feel her gaze burning into the side of his face.

Gary undoes his seat belt. He elbows into the space between the steering wheel and her chest and hits the autolock on her armrest. He opens the door and sets his foot down on the pavement.

"What will you do? Call up one of your old girlfriends and see if she'll give you a ride?" Roz has her sunglasses on though the day is grey and sloppy.

"What's that supposed to mean?" Gary asks.

"Don't be stupid," she says.

Ah, he thinks. *And there it is again.* Lurking in their conversations like a butcher knife at the bottom of the dishwater. His extra life, snug and seamless, has caught on the keen edge of Roz's attention. Roz *knows* – though she can't prove a thing. She smells guilt on his breath, on all his clothes. Other women. Sidelines and diversions. They roll around in his thoughts like foreign words, like the crimes of other people.

Roz says, "If you get out now I'll circle around the corner. I'll hunt you down with my bumper."

Gary looks down at his shoe, shaped like a sock to the contours of his foot, the soles full of rubberized bubbles. Roz looks forward to meeting his mother – perhaps a little too eagerly. Until right now he hadn't understood. She intends this trip as a form of punishment, a domestic squeeze play. He returns his foot to the inside of the vehicle and slams the door with a careful crash. He'll have to maintain. He's going to need Roz for the moral support, for the holidays that lay ahead.

Roz gives him some cut-eye, then swings her gaze back to the road. She shifts from park back to drive, and they're moving once again. The lampposts have been decorated with giant silver bows. Kids walk around with their hoodies up as if they'd never be caught dead carrying umbrellas.

They drive over the mountains, the divide between east and west, then and now. On the downslope they whiz through cool pockets of ancient, shaggy trees. The land flattens. Grassy ditches and trailer homes with smoke chugging out of hatted pipes.

They enter the town of Gary's childhood abruptly, travelling from forest to civilization in a single red light. The town is a discreet, unimaginative grid of split-levels with a commercial vein running down the main street. A community constructed with utility in mind, without cul-de-sacs or municipal gardens.

They make their lefts and their rights. They crunch up the gravel driveway and park behind his mother's vehicle, a Lincoln Town Car with a deflated tire and lapsed licence plates. The house, a yellow cube with four front windows, stands before them like a giant block of butter. It has a tidy quaintness to it. A quality that never aligns itself with Gary's memories.

Roz strides to the door with certainty of purpose. She doesn't even ring the doorbell. She steps inside, and the house swallows her up. Gary waits for a minute sniffing the wind, which blows around smells of the town both new and familiar. He goes in through the side door that leads through the garage. The front door was only for visitors.

Gary knows the textures of the house as unconsciously as he knows the pores on his own arm. The lumps in the wallpaper. The particular steps to the basement whose risers are higher than the rest. Every inch has been travelled by his fingers and trammelled by his feet. It's a jungle of knick-knacks. Move one thing, and the entire house becomes strange, as if clutter is the cement that holds it all together.

Together and apart, Gary and Roz go in search of his mother. They follow the roar of an electrical appliance straight to the kitchen. Their routes conjoin where the carpet meets the linoleum. They see Gary's mother kneeling on the floor, deep in the lazy Susan with the vacuum cleaner hose. She wears a housecoat and a pair of mock-athletic slip-ons. The two of them puzzle silently over how to approach without scaring her to pieces, without eliciting a heart attack.

"You," Gary mouths. "You go."

Roz scowls. She thrusts Gary by the shoulder into the corner.

Gary takes a step while deciding where on her back his hand should touch down. "Mom," he shouts. The scream of the vacuum goes on. It is an obnoxiously loud vacuum. One of those shop vacs that could suck a bird out of the air if pointed in the wrong direction. "Mom," he says again. What a strange onomatopoeic word. *Mom.* Couldn't there be a phrase more complicated, more fitting? But there isn't – hasn't ever been – anything else. He looks back at Roz, who rolls her eyes. She thinks he is pathetic. Gary follows the vacuum cord back to the wall. He yanks the plug and the pod goes silent.

"Oh, fuck a duck," says his mother from inside the cabinetry. Then she backs out, her body emerging like a squiggle from a tube. She presses herself upright with her hands on her knees and stares quizzically at the vacuum.

Gary says her name. Her body convulses. Her whole frame lifts an inch or two. She lets out a shriek.

"Gary," she cries, pressing her hands against the side of her head. She gives his shoulder a hard, corrective slap. "Don't ever do that." She begins to cry. A jagged spurt of tears that's over as quickly as it begins.

Gary is tall and lean. She is small and tough, like an old-dame actress, but with the hands of a man and tired pouches under her eyes. When they embrace she turns her head to the side – her chin doesn't reach his shoulder. There is a smell about her, both comforting and repulsive, the scent of his primitive memory. It has a brand, he was surprised to discover. A blue tub, a neat box. A smell with an endless life.

They come apart.

The kitchen is exactly the same with its fife-and-drum wallpaper and maize-coloured appliances. Its unwavering sameness defies Gary's eye. In the midst of all this his mother is shrinking. As her body dwindles her hair gets bigger. She wears, like defence, a wig. Whenever Gary looks at the crown of her head he sees stitching, like the warp and weft of a carpet. Who knows what's underneath? Now she wears dentures, toothy new teeth – whitely optimistic, equine. Creepiest of all is a plastic port, installed in her chest, leading straight to her jugular for the easy injection of drugs. These artificial body parts have crept up on him somehow. Moved in between his visits and made themselves at home.

Something is wrong. But the wrongness, with time, has turned normal. The crumbling teeth, the fallen hair. It's not the sickness in the end but the cure that does the damage, the battering ram of modern medical repair. The disease is altogether different. Something sneaky and mutant and tough to nail down. He can't even mention its name.

Now Gary's mother dabs at her eyes with the cuffs of her housecoat. She says, "I didn't think you were coming until lunchtime." This is the stuff she cries about – lateness, surprises. The lack of cheese sandwiches, unmade beds.

"It's Roz's fault," says Gary. It serves as introduction. "She wanted to leave at the crack."

Gary's mother smiles wanly and shakes Roz's hand with the ends of her fingers. Sensing weakness, Roz relaxes. She moves in to attack with kindness. An awkward little hug and a check-to-cheek kiss. Their trip over was brilliant! They are thrilled to be invited! Because, in public, this is what Roz does best. She pumps air into moments until they are lighter and happier than ever, like blimps tied to parade floats.

Gary watches two parts of his life collide, small yet large, like atoms in a particle accelerator. His mother disentangles herself and shuffles a few steps backwards. She eyes Roz dubiously. It pleases him. He's afraid of what they'd talk about if they ever got the chance.

In preparation for the mess of Christmas, first there must be cleaning. Roz and Gary's mother agree to it telepathically, circling, scouring in tandem, like two dogs beating prey out of the underbrush. They don't even know one another, but he supposes this is how they will bond. Domestic science, rituals of polish and cleanser.

Gary flips a magazine on the living-room couch. He overhears Roz ask, "Do you have Pledge?"

"Pledge? You don't need that stuff. Just a cloth and some elbow grease."

In the evening they eat salad. Iceberg lettuce, anemic tomatoes, soft shavings of marbled cheddar. A few games of cards. Gary and Roz tell about their jobs like prodigal travellers, toting the world to the door in their pockets. Gary's mother turns her chair towards Gary and her back to Roz. She dishes the town gossip, avoiding any mention of unhappy facts – the suicides, obituaries, the messy divorces. She sounds like a narrator, like someone left out of the action.

Before bed Roz and Gary rendezvous in the bathroom. Gary pulls the shower curtain back and stands, dripping, in the steam. Roz brushes her teeth at the bathroom sink.

The room is coral pink. The bath mat, the toilet seat cover. The towels. Pink and shaggy, like the fronds of anemones. There are a million kinds of product. Solutions, lotions, oils, conditioners for the hair and skin. His mother has furnished the bathroom with enough emollients to moisturize Saudi Arabia. Even the towels. The towels are so soft Gary finds it difficult to get dry.

Roz peeks inside the medicine chest and then quickly closes the door. Gary glimpses prescription bottles, gauze pads, a length of surgical tubing that sends a shiver down his neck.

"Her skin is very sensitive," Roz tells him importantly.

"How do you know?" Gary asks.

"You can tell by the way she moves in her clothes."

"Why are you so interested? Why do you tell me these things?"

Roz devours every little detail. Gary can't bring himself to look. Roz and his mother are not even relatives, not yet. Not even close to blood.

In the mirror, naked faced, Roz looks vigorous and pink. She wears one of Gary's miscellaneous corporate T-shirts. Gary steps onto the bath mat. He wants to get closer, to squeeze Roz clean of her tingly glow and smear it all over the house. He kneads her shoulders and presses his nose into her hair. Shampoo.

Roz spits into the sink. His hands travel down. He slides them under the shirt and down the back of her underwear.

"You feel nice," he whispers dirtily. "Squeaky clean."

Something has come over him. It must be the holiday, the reprieve from the crush of routine. He feels, abruptly, like mating with Roz, like impregnating her, against his mother's pedestal sink. It's something else, too. He's hiding out.

Beyond the door Gary's mother hovers. Up and down the hallway in slippers. There is a soft knock on the door. "Knock, knock," says his mother. As if it's a joke, her uncanny household omniscience. The end of his sexy fun.

Roz slips away to the ends of his fingertips and pinches her contact lenses from her eyes.

Nothing much about his room has changed from his teenaged years. The closet is full of petrified soccer cleats. Boys' magazines, earnest in their geeky, asexual pursuits. Clothing on hangers sheathed in plastic wrap. The walls are faux-walnut panelling.

He and Roz lie in Gary's former bed. Roz complains that they won't sleep well, the bed is too narrow. But it's the way he likes it. Too tight, everyone shoved into close proximity. His mother in the next room. He and Roz lying right on top of one another. He feels a mental snugness, touched on all sides by his women. He feels like a teenager with a girl smuggled into his bed, like he's fooling everybody and no one, not even himself.

Roz says, "She hates me."

"She doesn't hate you. She only just met you. And she's not an easy person to know." But Gary doesn't want to think about his mother. He can hear her beyond the wall engaged in some unspeakable late-night puttering. Water in the bathroom sink. Liquids poured into the toilet from a height. He wants to fixate on Roz, his healthy, nubile girlfriend.

He rolls over onto his side and begins massaging Roz's back. Her shoulders are tight, the muscles stringy with knots. He kisses her neck, which she allows him to do, her body flaccid with begrudging acceptance. It's okay to pummel for therapeutic purposes, but when his hands begin to soften and linger, she shrugs them away. She twists her neck and slays him with a look that's like an icicle jabbed into his chest.

Roz never wants to have sex anymore. When she does it's in an air of fake Victorian sacrifice. Now she says, "Sometimes when I can't sleep I look at you next to me, lost in your oblivion. I think, my god, what am I doing here? I can't look at your face without wanting to punch it."

"Have you ever punched anyone in your life?"

"No."

"Not even siblings?"

"They don't count."

"Excluding siblings."

"No," she says. "I've never hit anybody. But I can imagine it could be quite satisfying."

"I've punched someone."

"Of course you have," she says snidely.

"What's that supposed to mean?" He lets out an irritated sigh, wanting to get it all over with. He wants to get them in and out of Christmas, home in one piece for the New Year's parties. He wants them – all three of them – to be normal again.

"You're the one who likes to get dirty, but you always come out smelling clean." Then Roz rolls away like a burrito, taking the covers with her. Her formidable shoulders protrude from the armholes of her tank top. White cotton, butchy, made to look like a man's. *A wife-beater*, thinks Gary.

It occurs to him that Roz prefers this mood of suspicion. It's easier to be wronged and right.

In the morning they drive for an hour to a neighbouring town made of malls.

Roz does not know how to pack for small towns. She dresses elegantly, resentfully, in black. She leads the way in her pointy-toed boots through the crowds in the mall with great assurance of her own mighty style, like an icebreaker. Gary shepherds in the rear. Wherever Roz goes, she walks fast. The soles of his mother's shoes flash before him, hard at work to keep up.

They pause on the escalator. "So. What do you want?" Roz asks.

"I don't know," he says. It occurs to Gary that he hasn't yet bought either one of them a gift. Gary avoids asking Roz what she wants for fear of how much it will cost.

His mother says to Roz, "Gary doesn't like surprises."

They laugh darkly at his expense. Roz is thrilled by the accidental alliance. She takes his mother's hand off the rubber rail and holds it. Gary's mother slides her hand out of Roz's, without looking her in the eye. The slippery, sleight-of-hand way she has when faced with anything she doesn't wish to do.

Mid-thoroughfare carts spangled with assorted throwaway crap. Kids with backpacks and drinks in food-court cups jostle Gary's elbows, forcing him to change course. *Teenagers*, Gary thinks with a sneer. He bumps back, like a hockey player, like a big bruiser.

The Bay sign glows at them like a yellow beacon signifying domestic wholesomeness, a shopping experience from deep in Gary's past, when his mother came for what she wanted and paid in dollar bills. Quality and ease and escape from a gazillion choices.

They penetrate the department store. It's no calmer, just slightly more expensive. His mother, who doesn't get to

malls often, is lured out of formation by the many entice-
ments. Cubes of cake on toothpicks. Beauty scientists in mint
green lab coats slather her wrists with gunk. Gary hooks his
mother in by the elbow and steers her back on course. She
smiles up at him and sighs, then tips her head against his
shoulder.

He isn't sure what to call the section they end up in, but
everything is breakable. Everywhere there are females. Old
women in ancient wool examining fragile, shiny receptacles
for the kitchen and dining room. Young women with glossy
hair, nice thighs packed into tight pants, breasts rolling under
sweaters every time the merchandise is turned over, price
tags checked, returned to the shelves. Who are they shopping for so methodically and exactly if not themselves? Gary
heats up under his jacket.

Roz and Gary and his mother. Their desires pull them
apart. They meander in the store, according to the lure of objects, like the points of a shifting triangle. Gary watches Roz,
pretending not to know her, asking himself, would he find
her attractive? Would he want to chase her down? Roz studies a kitchen gadget made from stainless steel. She almost
wants it, he can tell by the glistening in her eyes, but not
quite. It's not quite good enough for Roz.

Gary's mother is less hunter, more gatherer. She moves
down the aisles with faint aimlessness, her basket filling
with random consumer comforts for which she has no use.
Gary catches her eye. He watches her come closer and closer
until she is standing underneath him, like a bonsai in the
shade of an evergreen. She leans against him, looking up, her

pupils in a glaze. There is a film of sweat on her upper lip.

"Enough of this madness," she says. "I need to sit down."

He looks down at her hand on his arm. The meaty knuckles, the knob that is the pad of her thumb. He marvels at the robustness and frailty. He takes her basket from the crook of her elbow. "Don't move," he says. "Let me look for a chair." Where is Roz? Roz can cope. His feet bear him away.

He scans the vicinity for his girlfriend, for sales assistants, and finding neither moves off to farther reaches. He glances down at the objects in the basket, wondering how much will end up under the tree with his name written on it. He thinks of the Christmas tree, or lack of it. His mother's living room has gone fallow, the TV broken, the chimney unswept, no reason to sit there at all.

Gary spots a salesgirl in a Santa hat. She hurries, making way from one side of the store to another. He follows her, his attention snagged on the back of her short red skirt, her tights printed with candy canes. He catches up, pushing into her perfumey wake.

"Ho ho ho," says Gary. This is how Gary shops, neither like Roz nor like his mother. Interested only in the things that aren't for sale.

She rounds the shelving, slowing just enough as she corners to give him a long, amused blink. Scissoring legs, a long mane of scrunched hair. The sudden distraction, the instantaneous jolt. From behind she is neither young nor old. It doesn't seem to matter.

As Gary follows her across the floor it turns into a kind of game. She keeps walking at an athletic clip, pretending she hasn't already seen him. She adds a swish to her hips. A white plastic card swings back and forth on a coil at her wrist. She has the muscular calves of a runner. They flex and soften, flex and soften. "Wait," Gary calls. She pushes through a swinging door marked Employees Only. He sees from the profile of her face that she intends for him to follow.

Inside she is waiting for him, hands on hips. It's dark. Cardboard boxes and bubble wrap on the floor. A small round table with salt and pepper shakers, crackers in plastic wrap.

"Do we know each other," he asks, "or is it just my imagination?"

She says, "I don't know you from Jack."

There is always something faintly antagonistic to these encounters. The women are always a little bit angry with him for allowing themselves to be caught. But it's not just the sex he's after. It's the yes. The acquiescence. The rest is merely follow-through.

Here, in the backroom of Santa's workshop, which is seamy and cluttered, is where the real work gets done. A washroom with a light on, a mop and a yellow bucket on plastic casters. She sees him looking at the open door. Her hands are bedecked with rings. He makes his move around the table. She dances lithely away.

She lets herself be cornered between the sink and the wall, against a Gloria Estefan poster. Their bodies make contact. He can feel the press of her breasts. He slides his hands up her thighs and arrives at the control top of her pantyhose, where the flesh is squeezed tight under nylon. Her fingers meet his, the skirt in between. They shoo his hands down and away.

"Wait," she says. "Kiss me first."

As soon as he kisses her he decides he doesn't really want to. Her mouth tastes like peanut butter and cigarette smoke. He should be melting down from his mind and into her body, drifting off to a mental Tahiti. But there is product in her hair that makes it feel like Easter grass. Obstacles in the form of bra hooks and pantyhose, bureaucracies of anonymous desire.

She backs up and her face contorts, and she sneezes into her hands. And with that their connection stretches and breaks and floats like a thread to the ground. His hands fall away.

He slides his cuff up on his watch and asks, "How much time have you got?" Nothing is as natural as it seems like it could be. They are simply trying too hard.

She looks a little bit crestfallen, as if he's failed her in some small way. They button and straighten. He works hard to avoid her eyes. She flips her head upside down and fumigates herself with hairspray. They step out of the stock room back into the store, scanning for signs of trouble. But in the Bay everything's just the way they left it, cheerful, proper and bright. He moves apart from her, sidewinding across the floor.

She asks, "Don't you even want my number?"

Gary returns to where he left his mother. She isn't there. He wonders what he did with her basket, moving with a sense of semi-urgent confusion. Carpet passes under his feet. Squares of bright light cruise by overhead. He roams in a search-and-rescue grid until he hears his name over the PA.

They have carried Gary's mother to Linens and laid her out like a fairytale character on a daybed, a puff of eyelet and white cotton. Two of the staff hang over the footboard, like the dwarves. Roz sits on the edge of the bed with her hand, somewhat melodramatically, Gary thinks, behind his mother's head, feeding her sips from a bottle of water. Choral music rains down from perforated circles in the ceiling.

"What happened?" Gary asks. Though in truth he does not need to ask. He is merely buying himself time. His mother looks at Roz as if she hates to be a bother.

Roz takes a long moment letting her eyes get to him. Her eyebrows growl. "She fainted," says Roz.

They buy nothing in the end. Roz pushes through the glass doors. His mother squeezes out from the building looking stunned, shielding her eyes. She produces a crumpled plastic rain bonnet from her purse and spreads it gingerly over her hair. Roz scans right and left for the car, slow and deadly, like the Terminator.

They pack his mother into the back seat as if she is a science-fair project gone bad. Roz says *okay?* and *all right?* a lot. Gary guesses there's a cost attached to all her doting and nursing. A price she'll exact later. It's his own fault. He lets everything get too convenient.

Roz clicks herself into the passenger seat and says nothing. Gary shunts them out of the parking lot into a blockage of cars. In the rearview, his mother stares out the window with her cheek in the cup of her hand. Tail lights and puffing exhaust. Cars are jammed floes in a river of traffic. He brakes and accelerates vigorously to let Roz know that he, too, is in a foul mood.

Roz glares at him in the red glow of tail lights and asks, "Where the hell were you?"

He catches his mother's glance in the mirror. She looks between the two front seats and arches an eyebrow. He's made the mistake of underestimating her.

They are back home. His mother looks grey. They did it together, he and Roz. Wore her out together but separately. Roz with her habitual zip, her neurotically fast-forward pace, Gary with his taste for the lurid and dangerous.

"Cup of tea?" Roz asks. She offers every beverage available in the refrigerator. Every comfort in the house. Blankets, hot water bottles.

"No, no," says Gary's mother. "Nothing."

Roz makes the fuss anyway, some new-agey herbal Valium drink imported from their cupboards at home. She slides the mug towards his mother like an expert, a pusher. "I always drink this whenever I'm feeling terrible."

Gary's mother sits at the kitchen table looking glumly down into her beverage. She sniffs the steam and says, "Well, dear, that's lovely. But I won't have any just now." No cup of tea is going to fix what she's got.

She waits until Roz and Gary have turned their backs, and then she slips off to her room. The way she has always gone to bed – stealthily, without a word of goodnight.

Gary and Roz stare at the sloping ceiling, pebbled and white, their breath roiling between them. Before retiring, Gary tossed back a few gulps of brandy directly from a dusty bottle atop the china cabinet. Now it wafts around on his breath. Roz drinks neither coffee nor booze and resents it when anyone else does.

"Don't give me shit," he says. "You're the one who ran her around the mall."

"She passes out and you evaporate?" Roz sounds like she's taking everything personally, like he's flunking a pre-marital exam. She turns her head on the pillow to peer at him. "Where did you go, anyway?"

"Please," he says. "I'm not good with this stuff. Flat tires, yes. I can fix your laptop when it dies."

"This is not a Future Shop purchase. This is your mother." Believing, if the tables were turned, she'd be bedside, right there with the hot towels and the Vapo-Rub. It's because she doesn't have to. Her own mother is vigorous, resplendent with good health. She snowboards on winter weekends, has biceps shaped like potatoes.

He flips over, throwing his head down on the pillow. "Why don't you go find yourself another, better guy?"

"Oh no," she warns him. "That would be too easy." She presses herself against his spine. "I want you, with modifications."

"But I'm just this."

"A *cheater*." Her whisper is a hot puff in his ear.

Roz has been toying with him like this for weeks. Sniping at his feet from the rooftops, relishing his panicked dances.

For this he'd like to teach her a lesson. He'd like to stretch her out over the mattress and do it her, in the site of his tortured adolescent yearnings. *Do you like this? Am I a good boy?* He gets half an erection just thinking about it.

Gary wiggles down out of his shorts and snaps them across the room. Roz armours herself against the impending overture by rolling over and pressing close to the wall. She lies with her forearm stuffed under her neck, her fingers poking out from her hair. The resolute look of the back of her head sends a lustful shimmer down to the soles of Gary's feet and up the front of his body.

He begins by nudging himself against her back, wrapping his limbs around hers. He feels the stubble on her legs and the heat of her back. Next he works his hands into the bony valley between her breasts. He pushes along her ribs and even into the spaces between them. As if he could prod his way into her chest, into the deep tissues, and discover what she's hiding underneath.

"Ow," she says, "*ow*." Was that the real Roz, the woman he first met? Or was that false advertising for the Roz he's got here, scowling over her shoulder, pinned under the weight of his thigh?

Gary shifts himself on top of her in an attempt to pin her down to the mattress. She resists, wedging her elbow between their chests. Roz is a sturdy woman, stronger than she looks. Immovable, when she wants to be, as an Easter Island head. It's the part of her he hates to love. Someone to escape from, yet a body to ram up against.

He lowers his face to hers and kisses her on the lips. She

says to him out of the side of her mouth, "You didn't even shave. Your face is like broken glass."

They lie like this for several long minutes, tangled in an awkward embrace. Roz turns her head to stare at the wallpaper. She makes a visor of her hand. It's a strange kind of foreplay when she doesn't participate. He feels as though he's wrestling with a key in a stubborn lock. It turns slowly, and yet all at once.

They don't make love, not exactly. Among the sporting ribbons and model rockets and the plastic bags full of coat hangers. They make not a shred of noise. In his bed with a headboard scratched with initials, its Luke and Vader stickers. He thrusts himself in as if he could find himself inside her, as if he could fuck his answer out.

Once finished, they lie with the covers strewn around their limbs.

"See?" he says, panting down onto her face. "If I was good, you wouldn't even want me."

She replies, "You have garlic breath."

They flip onto their backs, drift to separate edges of the mattress. He pushes close, his nose into her hair. His arm falls tentatively across her chest. He listens to the in and out of her deepening breath as they drop down into unconsciousness.

Gary sleeps in. Not just a little bit but flamboyantly, long after Roz has left the bed. He gets up and bumbles around, reminding himself of how coffee is made in his mother's kitchen, for lately there are few signs of food preparation. No butter knives, no crumbs. The countertops are bare.

Little heels knock against the floor. His mother comes into the kitchen wearing a wool dress and gold earrings in the shape of macaroni. Gary whistles.

"Hot date with the postman?"

She smiles tightly, flitting around in a search for her house keys. He can hear the nervous multilayered rustle of her clothes.

Roz comes in. She hits him with a look of disgust. "You've got pillow marks on your face," she says.

"Why is everyone dressed up?" Gary wonders. He rummages in the cupboards. "Is there a funeral?"

"Are you looking for coffee filters?" Gary's mother asks busily. "They're on the shelf above the refrigerator."

It's as if they are preparing for a major mission to Mars. Tote bags filled with a neck pillow, cans of club soda, sandwiches in plastic wrap, a hardback book titled *Ladykiller*. Gary's mother is in love with soap operas, *People* magazines – cheap, fictive thrills. On the cover of this novel is a woman in tight pants, a suited man's hand spread over her ass. Gary sinks into this photo momentarily, finding a comforting seaminess in the stretched white pockets, the gem-studded pinky ring.

In life it seems Gary is destined to behave badly. His mother is merely fascinated with the lascivious bungling of others. She likes to terrorize herself with sex and romance. It gives her permission to feel superior, reasons not to fall in love again.

"Okay," says Roz to Gary's mother. How Roz loves to mobilize, to rush to the rescue. It makes her feel worthy, important. "Are you ready?"

Gary stands uselessly in the middle of the floor. His mother slides herself into her coat. She flashes the lining and flaps the lapels, making a big production of buttoning herself up. She snaps her purse clasp shut and feeds her arm into the loops.

"There's no cream," she apologizes. "Only skim."

"Where are you going?" Gary asks.

"Could you move the TV out of the living room? There's no place for the Christmas tree."

In the more dimly lit regions of his mind Gary knows exactly where they are going. To see Dr. Trimble. Gary's mother's good-looking specialist with the foreign accent and the hand-rubbing tic. *Dr. Moneybags*, thinks Gary. He takes appointments on the day before Christmas.

"Can't you wait five minutes?" Gary asks. "Let me put on some jeans."

"Don't bother," Roz says in a frosty way. "You just leave it to me."

They head for the door. Gary leans over the banister to watch them go. Roz exits last. She has a way of slamming a door without making a sound.

Gary returns to the kitchen. He probes through all the cupboards. He finds Corelle dishware in symmetrical, matching stacks. Special K, cans of Whiskas, vegetable crackers and Tetra Paks of tomato soup. That is all. He opens and closes the doors. The same ones, twice, three times.

In his mother's house an indolence overtakes Gary, a regression to the vestigial habits of adolescence. Rampant eating and interminable naps. Unapologetic mess-making. Now he slouches back to his unmade bed and lies down again. When he wakes up the day is hard-cooked. The women have not yet returned.

In his mother's house there is nothing to do, nothing to eat, nothing good to read. He visits the undersea bathroom. He takes off all his clothes. He stares at himself forwards and backwards in the mirror. Then he goes over every inch of his body looking at suspicious moles, spots, errant hair. He combs his head, wondering if his hairline corners are growing. The more he works himself over, the more intent he is on the discovery of flaws, signs, bodily defeat. Finding nothing, he begins to feel terrible. A clenching in the pit of his gut, hunger swirled in anxiety.

Gary steps out into the hallway naked. From the walls Gary's mother has removed – slowly, imperceptibly, one frame at a time – the cross-stitches, Gary's high-school pictures, the collage of aunts and uncles. Snapshots like these are everywhere in Gary and Roz's apartment, like billboards along a highway. On the fridge, on the mantel, in the bathroom above the light switch. Gary with Roz. Roz with Gary. Sometimes touching, sometimes not. On display for anyone who isn't convinced.

All that remains in his mother's hallway is the Sears portrait of Gary's father. The eyes appear to follow Gary no matter where he stands, like an image of Christ. Only it's his dad with his begrudging beaver-toothed smile. A western shirt with a ballpoint pen sticking out of the breast pocket. Gary squares off with the face, staring until the photo pixelates and the features fall apart. The great spool of time unravels. Two things in the world made Gary's father happy, and neither of these was a person. He loved meat. Gary's mother used to wield a sharp, glinting cleaver for hacking apart chickens and big hunks of beef. His father died young, a stranger. An erasure. A lifetime of fat and gristle.

Gary returns to his room and dresses, feeling translucent around the edges. It has something to do with the house. The walls have him in their inertial grip. He begins with several underlayers and ends up with his heavy coat on, at the door, the plastic hook of an umbrella in his hand. All the coverage he can get.

He lurks through the neighbourhood where the road shoulders into the gravel, for the sidewalks are few. No one in town walks anywhere. Even the kids are hustled around with their sporting gear in minivans and pickup trucks. On their parents' mud flaps, cartoon bad boys pull down their pants. A town grafted onto a logging camp, and even now most of it looks provisional, as if no one has any intention of sticking around. Mobile homes. Box-like bungalows with claptrap additions. Dwellings in denial.

The sky goes smudgy with afternoon dusk. He skulks down the hill towards the canal with a half-formed plan to get devastatingly drunk, to ruin his appetite for today and tomorrow. His mind burns a path straight to Roz. He'd like to waltz back in with another hickey on his neck and pee all over her arsenal of dangerous shoes.

When Gary returns – later, much later – he stops before entering the house to smoke a joint on the porch. The effect is paradoxical: he is deliriously drunk and yet crisply alert, so that each unfolding moment feels like a strange adventure in someone else's life.

He enters. A glow of light from the living room. Gary treads towards it, his hand skimming the wall. Reluctantly, inevitably, he proceeds into illumination, like a hapless character in a horror film, blind to what's around every corner.

Gary's mother lies crumpled in the recliner before the expired television set, as if engaged in the pantomime of watching it, her book splayed over the arm of the chair. Her eyes are closed. She looks like a decoy of herself, a blow-up that's lost half its air. Gary stops in his tracks. He holds his breath while waiting for signs, the comforting up-down of her chest. The TV has him in its deadened black eye. His pulse bangs, his heart in his chest like a cartoon character's, leaping to get out.

She comes to with a snort and rushes to straighten her glasses. "Oh, Gary," she says, covering her mouth, staring at the middle button of his coat.

The breath spills out of Gary in a hot, boozy cloud. The knot in his chest unties itself.

Her voice is gooey and tired. "Were you out getting some air?"

He sees they will enact the farce of pretending Gary isn't plastered, as they have since he began drinking at the age of fourteen. Otherwise, like Roz, she'd have to ask questions, receive answers that aren't to her liking.

The room wobbles under his feet. The air is pungent with the afterscent of a doctor's office. Medical updates, breaking news, the untold facts of the day.

A sleeper disease with a lackadaisical schedule. He wishes, every day, he could hurry its progress, to sweep everything along to its inevitable end. Not for inheritance or mercy but for the sake of his own comfort. All bombs to go off, the deal to be done. He'd prefer suicide, tragedy, to the long, slow slide. But that's never the way it happens. His mother is as resilient as a duck in a shooting gallery. Knock her down and she pops right back up again.

Her hand wavers out towards him. He takes it. The palm is spongy and cool. "Where's Roz?"

"In bed. Why aren't you?"

"I'm not tired."

"She thinks you don't like her."

"I like her," says his mother. "Well enough." She's always thought of his girlfriends like red tape — hassles to push through in order to get back to the goods.

"Why don't you want to go to bed?" he asks. Though he knows. She hates the loneliness of insomnia, the relentless look of the ceiling, the dark, circling thoughts. But this isn't right — a living room, a synthetically upholstered chair — it's too paltry, too plastic.

Gary comes around to the front of the chair where her feet are crossed on the rest. "I am going to tuck you in." He extends his arms to her. She looks at his hands, first one, then the other, as if he is asking her to drive drunk with him to the edge of the island and barrel right down into the Strait. He applies his knee to the footrest. It budges down into the chair.

"Don't be scared." What's underneath the wig? Dry skin and hairlessness, webs of pulsing blood vessels. How can he ask her not to be scared, when he is more terrified than she is? Their moment is coming, lurching around the corner. How will she require him, when the time comes? Bedsores, suppositories, fluids swirling down the drain. The job will be his alone.

Gary pries up each of her fingertips, her nails dug into the upholstery. There is rain on his coat. He is unreasonably, swayingly drunk. His mother turns her grimacing face into the chair's wing. He stretches her out by the arms. Before long she dangles from his hands like a small orangutan, stunning him with her lightness. She lets out a terrible whimper. It's a mistake what he's started, but there's no going back. Parents with small children must come to know this. He thinks of baby primates, locked onto their mothers' fur. They flee through the jungle from hunters and enemies, born clinging, not knowing how to let go.

Gary creeps into his bedroom feeling flayed by the impotence of the day. He looks down at Roz where she lies in a ball, on her side, with her fist against her forehead. As soon as he clicks the door shut she snarls up out of feigned sleep, reaching for the lamp. The room fills with cozy, unwelcome light. They squint. Roz props herself up on both elbows.

"You stink," she says. "I can smell you from here."

He strips down to his underwear, leaving his clothes on the floor in inside-out tubes. A sad pair of ancient underwear, with withered elastic and a drooping crotch. He stands next to the bed, scratching the back of his neck.

Roz says, "Find a tail to chase besides your own?" She's talking now as if she hasn't just woken up, as if she's been preparing for his arrival all day.

Under the covers, Roz is naked. Gary looks around the room for something to wear, some fabric to put between them. In his room, Roz has installed herself completely. He lifts up her sweaters and puts them back down. He looks behind her satchels and her bags-within-bags, her bottles of lotion and potion. Everywhere he looks, he can't find himself.

Roz peers at him icily. She tracks him around the room with her eyes. She says, "I spent my day in a clinic. All these decrepit people with their oxygen tanks and colostomy bags under their shirts. Everyone pretending everything's fine, everything's normal. While we were waiting I watched your mother shred a half a package of Kleenex. She was terrified."

Gary's vision tunnels down, its edges growing black and fuzzy. A looming, toppling drunkenness. He reaches down for the comforter's edge, but instead of climbing in next to Roz he yanks it from the bed. It slips sideways and tents down on top of her suitcase. Roz is left with nothing but the top sheet. She retracts her feet. He can see the shape of her body, her thighs curling into her chest.

Roz gets a funny look in her eye as though she doesn't care for Gary's tone. It's too dark and unacceptable. She looks almost scared, and he wonders if even that, too, is phony. She clings to the top edge of the sheet as if it can save her from something – their crumbling mutual future. He peels the bottom edge out from under the mattress, and then he starts to pull. Roz clutches tighter. They have a short tug of war, and then Roz lets go. White fabric sails to the floor. Then there's nothing between his eyes and her nakedness. Her white calves and painted toes and the soft folds of her belly.

He asks, "Where the fuck are all my clothes?"

"In the dryer," Roz says murderously.

When Gary wakes up, Roz isn't there.

Gary's eyes are encrusted. A headache gongs against the inside of his skull. He stumbles to the bathroom to grope for T-3s. He hears a car engine start. The bathroom window is frosted. It lifts only an inch or two. He presses his face to the gap, where a sliver of cold air brushes his eyeball. In the driveway, he sees Roz, backing out in her car. Behind the windshield, she swivels, her hand on the passenger's headrest. A curtain of hair conceals her face. Gravel sprays out from under the front tires, a moderate but angry feed, as if even that has been well thought out. In the road, she throws the car from reverse to drive while still in motion. Gears clunk down into place.

He skulks into the kitchen. His mother pauses at the kitchen sink with a teapot in her hands. He thinks he's just caught her in the middle of something.

"Where did Roz go?" he asks.

"I think she went on a quest for a turkey. She won't find one now. It's too late."

His mother lifts the lid and swings the tea bag into the

garbage can, then she dumps out the liquid into the sink.
She dries the pot with a dishtowel. She dries it so thoroughly
he wants to rip the towel out of her hands and strangle her
with it. When she's done with all this she moves on to the
next thing. She shoves the towel up into a juice glass, staring down into detergent rainbows.

A Christmas without gifts. Neither of them seems to care. In
the living room Gary's mother assembles a fake Christmas
tree. Its limbs remind Gary of Astroturf.

To make room, Gary removes the TV, a wood-encased
dinosaur with dials instead of buttons, and broken antennae.
It presents no handholds and is heavier than a safe. He carries it with shuffling desperation, unsure if he'll make it to her
desired destination. The cord comes trailing behind. Even it
has been ravaged, by the teeth of a now-deceased dog. His
mother circles him as he moves, holding open doors, saying
"Watch your step" and "Careful of your back."

The garage, an archaeological site packed with family
detritus. Rusty tools surround them. Tire chains. A monkey
wrench. Baby food jars filled with screws. Utensils for mend-
ing and building. She throws nothing away, not even the
recycling. Her intermediate zone between *here* and *gone*.

"Tell me where to put it."

"Hmmm," she says with her hand on her chin.

"Think fast," he groans. Fast is something that's never
come naturally. She chews slowly, thinks deliberately, always
chooses her words.

A muscle in his arm begins to twitch and fade. The TV slips out of his grasp. It lands on the concrete, screen down, with a muffled, boxed-in crash.

"It's like it just leapt out of my arms," says Gary. They stand for a while shaking their heads at the shrapnel. Gary turns the box over. Shards of grey glass dangle from the edges. Electrical guts, coloured wires, the open mouth of the tube.

"Oh well," says his mother. "Oh well." She reaches for a broom.

Gary reaches for an axe. He brings it down off the wall from where it hangs between two nails.

"Stand back," he warns her. Gary lifts the axe high above his head. It lands with a woody crash.

Gary's mother flinches. She beats a retreat, a sort of terrified moonwalk, towards the laundry door. "Gary," she gasps. "Your eyes!"

A square-shaped view of the oily, grey world. A dry square on the gravel where Roz's car had been sitting. A knob in his throat like a burl. His mother is a Jenga of twig-like bones. Disappearing in a crumbling puff. Swept up with a broom and a dustpan. The details, the details. The detestable lightness. The incredible stampede of time.

THE ART OF MEDICINE

Here was Anne, washed up on the shore of her future, peering up at a narrow Victorian with windows like punched-out eyes. She stood on the sidewalk in the shadow of the house while the cabbie removed her boxes and Rubbermaid bins from the trunk. Then he slammed the lid down, nodded to her and raced away. Anne watched him go. He was the only person in the city she could say she knew.

A woman came out onto the front steps. She was tall and beefy looking. Anne trickled up to meet her. The woman carried a white bowl of chocolate pudding. She stuck the spoon in her mouth upside down. It came out glinting and clean. She introduced herself as Colette. The sky was soupy with clouds. The leaves rustled in the trees. Colette shook Anne's hand like a man.

Together they carried Anne's boxes up to her new room. Anne stood in the middle of this off-white cubicle, looking around and scratching her head.

"Girl," asked Colette. "Is this all there is to you?"

A new city, a new wonderful life. Anne lost herself in the blur of newness.

The streets were a giant maze. She had to keep consulting her various maps. Everything was a chore, an expensive, time-consuming hassle. Where to find the bargains? Where to buy cheese?

Classes began. She dashed between them. The campus sprawled. She left far too early to find her way anywhere on time. Then she sat around like a fool on public benches, killing time.

She showed up to all the requisite surveys: Anatomy, Neurology and Behaviour. She and her classmates would start at the very top, her instructors informed her, with the human brain. Eventually they would break it all down. From the science of the mind to the intricacies of the individual cell. The ways in which the human body transacted the business of life. The ways in which it was invaded and taken over. From the Art of Medicine she would learn to listen to her future patients. She would absorb certain principles of compassion. From Medical Ethics, a sense of fairness and jurisprudence. How? How would they begin to teach her all that?

She would begin at the beginning, learning from macro to micro. Her professors spoke rapidly through microphones. Their faces were smears in the distance. They whipped transparencies around on overhead projectors. Numbers and formulae streamed before her eyes. She transcribed everything they said in flurries of scribbling. She sat in the lofty seats of lecture theatres, at a distance from her classmates, who seemed to know everything already.

Her bedroom smelled like fresh paint and fabric softener. The rest of the house smelled like food and dirty clothes. She hung nothing on the walls but a calendar. In this room, with the door closed, she lay on the bed like a formless, melting thing, with a textbook splayed on the floor.

The gorgeousness of the body. The elegant symmetries of musculature and skeleton. None of it matched by any machine, technology or creation of the human mind. Who cared? Each night she stared at printed words and waited for them to tell her something fascinating. In the morning she woke up with her head at the wrong end of the bed, forgetting where she was.

She had come from a neat undergraduate degree in a neat suburban place where the only things drifting around in the breeze were mown grass and the smell of new paving. Now, when she trudged home, it was through September drizzle with a tightness in her chest. The air was thick with rush-hour smog. She had headaches. Time moved too fast, dioramas of the future opening up with every step she took. People crawled the sidewalk like possibilities.

At the end of each day Anne returned to her newfound home only to find it strewn with half-finished projects, the rooms bursting with clutter. Colette had not bothered to make room for her. Not in the fridge, not in the cupboards, not anywhere. And yet despite the mess, the house was stone quiet. No one visited. It was cold – a malfunctioning thermostat.

Anne trod diplomatically, claiming territory with a dustpan and a broom, with rubber gloves and Comet. But the battle proved useless. The more she fought the chaos, the more it edged in like moss.

Anne cleared a space on the table with the back of her forearm and sat down to a plate of steamed vegetables and rice. Colette stood at the stove, cooking in a flurry of utensils and ingredients. The house stank of sausage and garlic. Tomato splatters coated the stove. Anne put a forkful in her mouth, chewed and then stopped, her back teeth clicking together. Wherever Anne went, she found strands of Colette's hair. It travelled on her sweaters and clung to the bottom of her socks. Now she pulled a long wavy tentacle from the side of her mouth. As the hair slid out she burned a smouldering hole in Colette's back with her gaze.

Anne threw her fork down on her plate. It snapped the silence in two. "This place is a fucking swamp," she said, her mouth ruined with the imagined taste of shampoo.

"If it bugs you," said Colette without turning around, "move out."

Anne stormed to the foyer and ripped her coat off its hanger. She banged open the door and let her own breeze carry her out.

She stomped the sidewalk in no particular direction, and by the time she reached the cinema her anger had steamed off the top. All she wanted was to sit in the dark and get sucked up in the flow of someone else's incredible, fictitious life.

She stood in the concession lineup with her hands in her pockets and a craving for salt and fat. She had a craving the size of the world. She gazed up at the menu and hoped she would figure out what she wanted by the time she reached the front of the line.

The man behind her, standing far too close, was tall as a tree. He talked into his cell phone, negotiating with someone who seemed to be annoyed with him. Anne took a step away, closer to the coat in front of her. He wedged himself into the space she had made, and then he stepped on her heel. Her shoe peeled away from her foot, the leather collapsing under the aggressive rubber sole of his boot. He continued to talk. She looked over her shoulder and strafed him with a look.

"Oh," he said, interrupting himself. "I think I stepped on your foot." He had a ragged haircut and a sharp black coat and he smiled in a way that made her even more furious. Anne could tell just by looking at him that he was the kind of asshole who barged into situations, expecting everybody else to get out of the way.

"Look." Anne pointed down to her foot. "You crushed my shoe."

He held his phone away from his ear. "Hmm," he said. "So it seems."

She felt she'd met his kind a hundred times before. She squinted up at him. His hair and his clothes, his size and demeanour. The more she looked, the more familiar he became. And before long Anne began to think she actually knew him, a suspicion she did not wish to investigate further. She hated coincidence, the intermingling of contexts. The past and the now, business with pleasure. She always felt as if she'd been caught behaving badly, wearing the wrong tatty clothes. Before the exchange could become a dialogue she whirled away and shoved herself forward in line.

His call was ended, the phone slapped shut. He loomed behind her, breathing down on her shoulders. She felt his presence like a fire at her back. When she reached the front of the line she was so unnerved she couldn't think of a thing to order. She asked for popcorn from a girl with braces and a golfing visor. Then she dashed away, the bag in her hand, deep into the darkness of the theatre.

Anne couldn't concentrate on the movie, which was sub-titled. She ate popcorn by the fistful, then chewed through each of the kernels at the bottom of the bag. She wondered if he had picked her at random and followed her in off the street. She thought about how she might know him.

After the movie he intercepted her en route to the door. He lifted her hand and kissed the air on top of it. "I am truly sorry about your shoe." His gaze skidded down her torso, then up again to her eyes. She felt nearly naked. Her wool coat, diaphanous. "You didn't like the movie, did you?" he asked. "I can tell by the look on your face."

"I don't like most movies," she said. Movies bored her. Everything bored her halfway through.

Strangers glided around them, leaving flesh-toned tracers at the margins of her vision, and it became abruptly apparent that this was her Ethics instructor, Dr. Julian Breen. A school with a gargantuan populace, which could be both a plus and a minus. Her professors kept their distance. Everyone kept their distance, and she could never recognize anyone up close.

He introduced himself as Julian.

The sound in the room crested into a low, coddled roar. He looked at her intently. The heat inside her coat was building, and soon she would have to take it off. Her body glowed. Her mind felt fast and alive. The seconds flew by with glinting edges, like the cars of a speeding train. She felt like throwing herself under the wheels.

He told her, "I know a place."

She said, "I'll bet you do."

They soared up in a high-speed glass elevator to the top floor of a downtown hotel.

"What's your name?" he asked.

"Anne," she said.

The bar was dark and decadent, upholstered in velvet, with Scotches and ports at stratospheric prices. She let him buy her an innocent drink, then two. And soon they were in deep exploration of the bar menu.

"Are doctors supposed to smoke?" she asked.

"No," he said. "But I'm not a *real* doctor."

And so, besides the movie, they had something in common.

"And you?"

"I do many things," she said. "But none of them well."

He drank fast. They talked fast. He put thing after thing in his mouth – nuts, stir sticks, cigarettes. He wore a wedding band. She stared until his hands disappeared under the table. Everything stratospheric, everything through the roof.

They leaned against one another on the trip down in the elevator.

"Do you have a boyfriend?" he asked.

"You're kidding," she scoffed. It was hard to believe he was an expert on the topic of informed consent.

They stepped out into the street, and the world had turned cold. The sky spat pellets of rain. They stood on the corner with their hands in their pockets, awaiting separate cabs. The streets looked greasy. A taxi zipped up with its white light glowing. She stepped towards it, and Dr. Breen caught her by the elbow.

"Kiss me," he said.

She unhooked her arm. "You have no idea who I am, do you?"

"No," he said. "Exactly."

He held the taxi door and she fell in and the night was suddenly over. Nothing left to do with her overripe head buzz and the stirrings of a crush but take them home and put them to bed.

She woke at sunrise to the roar of the vacuum. It was a sound and a time of day she couldn't associate with her roommate. Anne crawled out of her bed, still wearing her clothes. She crept downstairs. Her head felt like something thrown at a wall.

In the living room Anne shielded her eyes from the beautiful daylight, from the sight of Colette in her underwear. Who pushed the vacuum cleaner over and over a rogue strip of foil. She caught sight of Anne and shouted, "What the hell are you looking at?"

"Could you make a little more noise, please?"

Colette bent back over her task with renewed invigoration.

Anne yanked the cord from the wall. The vacuum whined down and was silent.

Colette glared. Anne put her hands on her hips and thrust her shoulders back. She could see Colette, who was almost a head taller, root herself into the floor. They stood in fuming silence until their squaring off felt ridiculous. The curtains were wide open. Colette wore underwear. You really had to love someone to want to pull their hair or scratch their eyes out.

Anne bent down and scraped it up with her fingernail. She stood and gave it to Colette, who crumpled it into a tiny ball.

Colette moped and muttered to herself all week. Anne went back to the task of memorizing body parts. Their paths crossed often despite the chilly mood. At every turn they blocked each other in doorways. The phone rang. No one answered it. Colette glared at Anne in her sulky way that seemed, underneath it all, to beg.

Anne could tell this much about Colette: She was the kind of person who thrived on admissions of guilt and ceremonious apology. She'd like the whole world to apologize. The kind of person who, if you swam out to her rescue, would climb on your head and drown you.

Then, when the week was over, Colette began to talk again. "You have a stalker," she said. Anne had messages. Three of them, piled up on top of each other. She listened to them all – once, twice and three times. Then she put the phone back down in its cradle.

Anne – a monosyllabic name, a name like a microdot, so nondescript you could overlook it. She was average height. Her hair was the colour of an animal that scurries in yellow grass and dirt.

Cloaked in averageness, she disappeared herself in the crowd of Dr. Breen's Ethics class. It was a huge section of a few anonymous hundred, mostly undergrads from Philosophy. Anne sat in the upper tiers of the auditorium and studied him from a distance. He wandered around on stage with his goofy, splay-footed, high-headed charm. He cracked lame jokes. Every fourth sentence he'd have to search his vocabulary for a word. Anne would pick one out and send it down to him like a telepathic paper airplane. *Incumbent*, thought Anne. Then he would say, "It's incumbent upon the physician to ask the relevant questions . . ."

No one thought he was cool except for Anne and the groupies. Women in slit skirts who sat in the front row so they'd have room for their knee-high boots, their pushed-up boobs and the waving of their stupendously long eyelashes. But Anne was not jealous. He toyed with their airheaded questions. Smiling, jingling the change in his pockets.

In the midst of these lectures she often lost track of the logic. Words sailed around her in useless circles. Anne peered down over the balcony to the heads of her fellow students below. Bald spots and cleavage. She experienced a strange compulsion to tip and fall forward, to whisper herself over the railing. She imagined herself like a sheet of paper, floating down into the dark spaces between their feet.

When Dr. Breen took his hands out of his pockets they were as big as flapjacks. Strong and long fingered and brown. She knew then something would happen. It was only a question of time. And waiting. As far away as possible – high, high up, near the rafters. A place, as in the mind, where no one was ever keen to look.

Colette was a graduate student in Women's Studies. When Anne had moved in, Colette revealed she'd been *thinking* about her thesis for five years. Anne wondered how anyone could *think* for that long. But within weeks, Colette had given up on her research, her teaching assistantship, everything to do with academe. She shrugged and asked of the air, "When is a test a sign?"

In lieu of university, she enrolled in a training seminar called The Power. After the first session, Colette came home with a crazy glint in her eye. She spread her handouts all over the floor. Anne knew they would stay there until Colette kicked them into the corner.

The gist of The Power, as far as Anne could tell, was this: They sang special songs and chanted certain mantras. A man, the big kahuna they'd paid to see, asked each participant one by one: What is the purpose of your life? They turned off the lights. They turned them back on again. His cheerleaders pumped the audience up. By the end of the course, he promised, everyone would have the answer.

"So what is it?" asked Anne.

"What?"

"The answer?"

"I'm still waiting," said Colette. She had just finished walking over hot coals without suffering so much as a blister. Now she was taking off her socks to prove it. "But I've never done anything so real in my life."

"Four thousand dollars," said Anne. "It better be real."

The phone rang. It was still early.

"Dr. Anne," Colette said archly, "the telephone is for you."

The handset travelled in slow motion from Colette's hand to Anne's ear.

"Why didn't you call me back?" Dr. Breen had a baritone that cracked in the middle when he asked certain questions. Anne liked it. It sounded a bit like grovelling.

Colette sat eavesdropping in bike shorts with her calf crossed awkwardly over her thigh. Anne turned her back and stretched the cord as far as it would go.

"Well," said Anne, "it's *you*."

"Meet me later," he said. Not a question but a command, as if it was medicinal.

Anne's ear burned against the receiver. "Where?" she asked. She glanced at her watch and then at Colette.

The phone found its way back to the hook.

"Girlfriend," said Colette, "it's a bad idea. A very bad idea."

They'd arranged a rendezvous at the hotel of their previous engagement. Anne wore her dowdiest pair of wide-bottomed underwear – as if it could protect her – and the fabric slid down on her hips with each stride she took along the sidewalk. She thought about her bank account. How she'd left it too long to get a job.

The hotel's buttressed awning rose up out of the concrete. She arrived at the brass doors but saw no sign of him. Four in the afternoon. The hour for affairs. She felt like a cliché, standing there, waiting.

Horns. Tires on pavement. Trucks backing up. All of these sounds bounced off the surrounding buildings, producing an auditory urban stew. The air was crisp. Anne could see her breath. People moved around in the windows of office buildings, busy at their work like bees in a hive. He was late. Or perhaps not coming. Nothing had happened and already her thoughts were a weird bouillabaisse of want and confusion.

Dr. Breen crept up behind her. He pinched her buttock through the wool of her coat and whispered in her ear. "You look delicious." She had to bend her neck back to look up at him. "Your lips are twitching. Are you nervous?"

"I'm *freezing*," she hissed.

All the leaves had come down off the trees. They nestled like crusts in the gutter. A day pushed right out on the ledge of autumn. Dr. Breen scrubbed her upper arms.

"Well, then. Let's go warm you up." He latched on to her hand and tugged her towards the massive old edifice that sighed hot breath every time its doors opened. The doorman was a woman who did what she was paid to do. Anne went through with her head down. In the lobby there were explosions of fresh flowers and carpets with vines that snaked up to the elevators.

.

She arrived home just after midnight with hyped-up senses, in love with everybody and no one. She walked up the steps, feeling the rail under her hand. The contours of chipped paint. The smell of garbage in the air.

Colette had returned from her seminar, with company. Colette introduced her guest as Ricky. She and Ricky sat in the living room sharing a polite beer out of little glasses, looking stiff and formal in their clothes. Colette sat trussed in a tight blue suit. Ricky wore a cheap white shirt and a knit tie. He had a thick neck, muscles of the kind men get from lifting weights in front of mirrors. He hooked a finger over his collar and tugged it down. Anne disliked him instantly. But why get protective about Colette? With her supersonic laugh and her feet squished into pointy new shoes.

"Ricky," said Colette, "this is Anne, my favourite person in the universe." Colette said this about everyone, and still Anne was stupidly touched.

Colette and Ricky continued their flirtation in murmurs. Anne climbed the stairs, riser after envious riser. The night had been strange. Her shutters blown open.

Anne was tired of searching for nutritious choices. She wanted to fall instead of climb, to be swept off her feet by obsession. A skidding, careening romance, the more torrid the better. She wanted to throw herself into the rapids just to see what the world might look like once she'd crawled out onto the bank.

But what did she love to do? She didn't know. The not-knowing made everything else – school, acquaintances, everything – seem like hideous tedium. Could she die from this particular kind of boredom? The unrelenting sameness of the day-after-day? Her instructors raced through their proofs and examples, omitting steps she hadn't learned but should have. The words she read slid through her mind without touching down. She'd rather fold napkins than be a physician.

Workgroups. Lectures. Modules. Learning packaged up like a Happy Meal.

At the end of a lecture, Dr. Breen returned marked papers. Students filed down the amphitheatre steps like ants towards a picnic. Behind his lectern a table was arranged with four stacks of paper, each containing a section of the alphabet. People fed themselves down and towards the centre – a mosh of bodies in jackets. At the very back of the lecture hall, Anne shrank down in her seat. Her paper was embedded in the third stack, but she didn't care about the grade. She could hardly remember writing an essay in the first place. *This is how it will have to be*, she thought. *Watching, from a distance.* She watched until the crowd began to disperse, and then she ducked out unseen.

The endocrine system. The Krebs cycle. Passive and active immunity. The lymphatic system. The complicated interrelations of the organs. How they worked and failed to work. The factory that was the human body. Lipids and proteins and osmotic gradients and pressure differentials and gaseous exchanges and fluids streaming through vessels. If you spread it all out on the ground it would be bigger than the AIDS quilt. But did it tell her anything about anything? She could get down on her hands and knees and scrutinize all these guts with a magnifying glass and still have nothing explained.

Their next meeting was a step down from luxury. He chose the Holiday Inn. They walked down a long, muffled corridor of numbered doors and peepholes. The room smelled of upholstery and plastic wrap. First thing, he crossed to the blinds and whipped them shut. In this temporary private darkness they could be in any city, anywhere on the face of the planet. His wife taught comparative literature at a university far, far away.

"Do you do this," she paused, "regularly?"

"Rarely," he said. "But you're special."

Uncanny that he'd picked her, his student, out of a city of a few million women. If only he knew just how special. As if some part of him craved a worst-case scenario, some demolition stirred into his boredom. She did. Maybe that's why they fit each other so well.

She fell against his chest, which was solid as a furnace. He smelled like expertise, like none of the guys she was used to with their attention deficits and their humongous plans for the future. Before she knew it he had backed her up against the wall. She stuck her tongue in his mouth. It tasted like booze. He bit her bottom lip. He stuck his hand down the back of her pants without bothering to undo the zipper. His hands roamed her all over. She felt dizzy, as though she was merging with the room. She closed her eyes. Vertiginous, flashing thoughts. When she opened her eyes again she'd slipped one leg out of her jeans and her underwear. They lay curled at her ankle.

They had done it once, and now they were at it again. Minus the flowers and the four-star bedspread. This time it was pure. It lacked a scent. He was close yet distant, replete with desire and repulsion. They did it as if they wanted to pulp something out of each other. It felt fantastic. Her pores stung. She wondered if he hated himself as much as she did.

Then they were done, panting and grinning stupidly. The lines of sweat trickled down the inside of her shirt, pulled by inevitable gravity.

Dr. Breen turned his head towards the door. His nose brushed the side of her face. "I think I'm in love with you."

"No," she said. "No, it's that I am in love with you."

Ricky dumped Colette. After all, who wanted an unstable isotope for a girlfriend? A woman who was constantly changing her clothes?

Colette cancelled her registration for the next installment of The Power, and now she had not even a single reason to get dressed. She swanned around the house all day in her thrift-store dressing gowns, her cleavage falling out of the front. She took bath after bath, draining the hot-water tank several times over. Her only guest was the acupuncturist. For him she lay naked on a sheet in the living room so he could stick her with his needles. Through all of this she wept furiously. She was a great gushing river. You could dam her up and power a city. The whole house was wet.

She sat buckled on the couch, surrounded by mounds of snotty, wadded-up tissue. Anne wanted to slap her.

"Give me a break," Anne cried. "You only went out with him for a month."

Colette's face dripped. She twisted and shredded her Kleenex. She looked up at Anne with red-rimmed eyes and sobbed, "I'm pregnant."

"Yikes" was all Anne could manage.

"Yeah," said Colette. "Yikes." She spread her arms wide and pointed down at herself. "Look at me. What kind of a mother would I make?"

Anne knew exactly the kind of mother Colette would make.

She slept in, badly. It wasn't the first time. She flung herself out of bed and threw on clothes and in the kitchen collected her hair into an elastic snapped from the newspaper. On the way out of the house the flapping edge of her coat caught a mug on the counter. It smashed on the floor. In her haste she left the shards right there. The splatter like a tea-beige Rorschach on the tiles.

A plague of parapraxis and forgetting. She kept missing appointments. Stubbing her toes.

The streets were bunged with idling cars. Two streetcars passed her by, full to the doors with arm-dangling passengers. Too late for patience, she jogged from her stop to the next. The air felt like a matrix of haste and obstacles and polluted exhalations.

Anne arrived at the door to the lab with its square glass window hatched into smaller squares by wire filaments. She pushed against the doorknob, the seal opened, and the room gasped with the change in pressure.

Her lab partners, two of them, sat on stools, puttering on their laps with paper and clipboards. They had just done a number on the gastrointestinal sections of a fetal pig and were now divvying the after-procedure.

"Sorry," said Anne. "The traffic." She could tell by their looks that her excuses bored them.

"Yeah," they said, fumbling their coats onto their shoulders. "We're done now."

"I'll do the write-up," Anne offered.

"The whole thing? It'll take you ten years. We have all the notes."

"You could email them to me," Anne suggested.

"Yeah," they said, scraping their stools back into place, inserting books and papers and writing utensils into the appropriate pockets of their backpacks. "We'll email you."

And then they were gone. Out the door with their bustling perfect efficacy, a superior junior-doctor unit. They left her alone in the room with its swabbed white floors and ventilation hoods and the gleaming patina of stainless steel. The surgical tubing, the Erlenmeyer flasks. The black tabletop still streaked with sponge marks. The rubbery preserved skin, the organs cold-cooked in formaldehyde. The deadly little cutting instruments. The latex gloves. How unyielding flesh could be. The smell. The *smell*. She did not want to see the insides of things.

Anne went down to the basement with the grit of dust and the creaky wood floors and the paint-encrusted pipes that ran the length of the ceilings. She wandered until she found a cold, cavernous bathroom with two toilets in high stalls. A bank of sinks where a woman stood making reparations to her makeup. Anne recognized this woman as the assistant to the faculty registrar.

Anne amazed herself in the mirror with the depth of her own weariness. The dark circles, the wan skin – each night she lay on her back and stared unblinking at the ceiling. She flipped and flopped on the mattress until the sheets were in a twist and the blankets had slipped to the floor. In the morning she woke up with gritty eyes, as if she'd crawled down a beach on her hands and knees. Her in-box was layered with messages from various instructors. Her absences had become "protracted." Her detachment from workgroups "conspicuous." They wanted meetings, explanation. She returned none of their calls. How could she, when her diet consisted of day-old bread and remaindered vegetables? Unopened envelopes accreted in the hall. She advanced cash on her Visa to pay her MasterCard bill.

The woman at the neighbouring sink applied an O of hot pink lipstick. Her name was Marcy, and she wore equally hot pink jeans. This colour was like a screaming against Anne's eyes. She looked away and then made up her mind. She was sick of being offended, sick of looking the other way. She was tired of one-sided visits and late-night calls. Of homework left undone. She couldn't listen to another word of praise for an absentee wife, another day spent being unsingle. She needed a life with the light let in, with room for tiny wonders.

She bent down over the sink and rinsed her cheeks. She brought her head up and blotted her face with an inadequate sheaf of brown paper towels. Their eyes met in the mirror.

"Are you all right?" Marcy asked.

Anne thought about this for a minute while her face dripped into the sink. "I am sleeping with Julian Breen," she said.

"Excuse me?" Marcy's hand wavered in the air, the nub of pink lipstick protruding from its tube.

"You heard me," said Anne. Sometimes the only way out of a bad situation was simply to make it worse.

In a few short weeks Anne would have to crawl up to Marcy's desk to beg for a signature on her emergency student loan form, but right now Marcy had no idea who Anne was. At home Anne had pickles and cheese in the fridge. There was a war on in the Balkans. People were being shelled on the other side of the planet, and here they were, she and Marcy, leaning over sinks to examine themselves in mirrors, trying to decide if they were pretty enough.

Anne went home. She filled a glass of water and gulped it down at the kitchen sink. *This is it*, she thought. *I'm crazy.*

It was a filthy madness. All the science. All the technology. She wondered why there was still no pill that would cure it.

Anne found Colette in the living room, in an armchair, rolling joints. She had them lined up like a row of bullets on the coffee table. She looked more sickly and bloated than ever. Her face fell into her hands. "I'm dying," she said. "Dying."

Colette told Anne how the smell of soft-boiled eggs nauseated her. Sounds of traffic in the street nauseated her. The colour of Anne's shirt made her stomach flip. The whole world was full of reasons to complain.

Anne asked wearily, "What are you going to do?"

Colette wrote down the address of her herbalist. She threw her car keys up in the air and expected Anne to catch them.

Behind the wheel of Colette's car, Anne studied the list of deadly sounding ingredients, black cohosh, lady's mantle. She drove across town with the list and her maps to a quadrant of the city populated by former citizens of the former Soviet bloc.

On the sidewalk she was met by three stout women walking abreast. They wore heavy flesh-toned stockings and carried string baskets full of bread. They came at Anne and pushed her off towards the parking meters. When they laughed their mouths glinted with gold crowns. The day was cold but sunny. How long had it been since Anne had stepped from her tight little routines? An uninformed sadness pulled at her gut. She thought about what it was like to live so far from home. She thought about what it was like to come from a country that kept changing its name.

Colette's herbal pharmacist, a gaunt, white-haired man, leaned in his darkened shop between a long counter and a wall of jars. Anne slipped the order across the counter. He read Colette's list, folded the paper, then shot Anne a look. He filled the order and, with a grunt, gave Anne a paper bag full of strange leaves and roots. These she carried back to the car as if they were something illegal.

At home Colette dumped the whole pouch into a pot and boiled it down to a dark, foul soup that stank up the entire first floor. The stench lifted her spirits. Anne watched her strain a glassful, hold her nose and choke the liquid down. She slammed the cup down on the counter and groaned.

Anne asked, "Are you a witch or something?"

She said she'd had some training.

Marcy worked in a building called Franklin Hall, which housed the administration for the faculty of medicine. These words were carved in granite above the entrance: VERITAS VOS LIBERABIT. The truth was setting someone free, somewhere. But not Anne, who entered the building feeling as if she were sinking in quicksand, being swallowed up by the floor.

Marcy and her co-workers made up an administrative collective, the kind of women who talked about liberal politics, then tabulated the length of each other's coffee breaks. They knew their own bureaucratic power, the clout in their very ink. Their desks were arranged open-kitchen style, each within eavesdropping distance of the next, behind a long and unbreachable service desk. Anne felt their eyes on her back. She could hear it in their voices, an inaudible hum in the air. The way they lost her paperwork, buried it in delay.

They talked – it felt as if everyone was talking – about her and Dr. Breen.

It wouldn't take Dr. Breen long to put his two Annes together, to join her face with a name on his class roster. Perhaps he already had. The waiting was an excruciating limbo. Days passed before her eyes like snippets of a grainy movie. Nothing felt real or in the least way significant. Yet the shards of her life were gliding together, on collision course, asteroids in deep space. Ripples would be felt. Cosmic dust would rain down. But the moments before were the most insufferable – full of hush and breathlessness.

Nothing happened, and yet everything hung. At home, the phone never rang. The phone was so silent Anne felt like smashing it to pieces.

She smuggled herself into Dr. Breen's class and sat high in the top corner of the mezzanine. She waited for him to come out from the wings with his books and flapping papers under his arm. Outside, beyond the windows, the grounds were strangely devoid of human activity. Young leafless trees scraped the wind. When he finally arrived, there were no more jokes. He prowled his way through his lecture, back and forth in a wide semicircle, hunting through faces in his crowd. At one point she even thought she felt his eyes flash over her. It made her want to raise her hand. To stand up out of the audience and shout down to him.

Her unclaimed essay had long ago ended up on the chalk rail. Dr. Breen had written her name on the board in block letters with a big white arrow pointing down like an admonishment. Now it was gone, her name smudged into the black by fingertips. The absence of this little white square in the distance filled her with hopelessness. She wondered how long it might take for Dr. Breen to forget all about her. But of course nobody forgot Anne unless she wanted them to remember, unless she needed them to feel haunted.

When class was done Anne sneaked out into the dilapidated hallway, the door slamming shut behind her. She stepped out into knife-edged sunshine. She descended stairs that had been worn into troughs by the feet of every student who had ever hunched over a book at the university. She stepped down, her eyes on the tops of her shoes, her mind in a swirl of disconnected thoughts. And she then heard her name. A little name, a big lie. She'd only just begun to feel the weight of it.

She didn't turn around. Her breath dropped down to the bottom of her lungs. But she kept walking, hesitating in midstep for a fraction of a second. When she heard the voice again she tucked her chin down inside her coat collar and pointed herself forward.

She walked quickly past the academic buildings and through the park, passing intangibly from the campus to the city at large. Her thigh muscles clenched, her whole body charged up with the gush of adrenaline. The sidewalks thickened with normal citizens, working people, out on their lunch-hour treks. She tried to lose herself among them, but she didn't slow her pace. Turning billboards, street lights, streams of moving cars. Her eyes skittered from shape to shape. And the whole time she felt him there, trailing a distance behind her.

When he called her name again his voice was nearly a bark. It travelled in a stiff wind that raked the trees and blew about scraps of paper. She broke into a jog. The soles of her shoes smacked the concrete. The wind plowed past her ears. But she was hardly athletic, her gait inefficient, and her shins began to burn.

She disappeared down the throat of the subway entrance, her feet cascading down the steps. At the wickets she was met by a great blockage of shuffling bodies, a human blob feeding itself slowly through the turnstiles. Anne fumbled in her change purse and pushed her way in. She shouldered to the front amid scornful looks, straining to free her coat from the press of bodies.

With her token in her hand and her knuckle on the slot, she couldn't help turning back. There was Dr. Breen, as she knew he would be, looming over the crowd like a tree in a flood, with his craggy face and strong brow and nose that jutted out like a hook. He looked at her and the light crumbled all around him, the stairs, the walls, the grimy green tiles. Anne felt the weight of a dozen people at her back. She had something to say, but her mouth had gone desperately dry. It could have been *sorry*, but it felt too late. The token had dropped, the turnstile had ratcheted, and there was nowhere left to go but through.

Days later, when she thought she might die of sleeplessness, she climbed aboard a streetcar in search of a different kind of ending. She had smudgy circles under her eyes. She had ten dollars in her pocket and a throbbing in her forehead. She had the reckless intention of visiting Dr. Breen's house, a bodily craving like the need for a drug, an appetite for obliteration. It pulsed stronger and more insistent with every block she travelled. The sky darkened as the streetcar lurched from stop to stop. It was the season in which the nighttime nibbled up the best parts of the day.

Dr. Breen lived where she expected him to live, in a more expensive, better-situated version of the house she and Colette occupied. She crept up to his door like a reptile, a slinking, slow-blinking lizard. She pressed herself out of the cone of porch light and waited for the neighbours to roll out of their driveway. She stuck her finger onto the doorbell. It gonged deep inside.

He took an outrageously long time to answer the door, and in this hanging moment a mild, peculiar terror began to rise up in her chest.

The door opened. A wedge of light fell across her face.

Dr. Breen blinked at her, alarmed. He hadn't shaved and looked somewhat like a criminal. She opened her mouth but before she could say anything, his finger shot up to his lips. He looked over her shoulder onto the street, then over his own shoulder into the house. Then he yanked her inside by the forearm. It reminded her that she hadn't been invited.

Anne closed her eyes and words began to dribble out. He clapped his hand over her mouth. She could hear his breath passing in and out of his nose. She imagined she could hear it deep in his lungs, could feel his pulse through the pad of his thumb. They waited and listened, for what she didn't know.

Dr. Breen led her into the house. The halls were tubes of pristine white. Halogen lights. Everything muffled and white, like a street covered in snow. Everything elegant and refined. If Anne had money she'd buy the same things. She wondered if that was his reason for choosing her.

They darted past the living room where the TV bubbled with music. Music of a genre Anne couldn't reconcile with the household aesthetic. She dug her heels into the carpet. Dr. Breen dragged her along by the wrists. Then she caught a glimpse of a girl – a teenager – lying like a mermaid on the floor, washed in cathode light. They rounded the corner. Anne stopped in her tracks. "You have a *daughter*?" As if a daughter evened their score, as if their scores were worth evening.

He turned abruptly and hissed down at her, "If you say another word I am going to kill you." He dropped her hand, and she fumed silently up the stairs behind him with her arms in a twist across her chest.

"Wait here," he said once they were inside his office. He gave her a cigarette, though she didn't smoke. Then he shut her inside and went back downstairs.

She sat down in his desk chair and its creaking edged through the silence. She examined the spines of his books, his paperweights, his pens. This was the desk of a man who owned furniture that looked like sculpture. Who left red-wine rings on the blotter. This was a man with paperwork mounded on his desk. Downstairs Anne heard the shuffling of bodies, the door opening and closing. The car engine revved. She stared at the texture of the paint on the wall and twirled the cigarette in her fingers.

A masculine womb of work and gravely important intellectual toil. In his absence she rolled his desk drawer open and picked through everything inside: business cards pencilled with jottings, Visa receipts. She even sniffed the pages of his books. His wife had a name Anne couldn't pronounce, not even in her thoughts, and it was there, written on a Post-it and stuck to the telephone. The wife in the photo with her ash-blonde hair and her beguiling gaze that tracked Anne no matter which way she turned. The photo frame stood on a pressboard leg. She gave this limb a flick with her finger. The frame fell down backwards and slipped behind the desk with a clatter.

Dr. Breen's car hummed back into its slot, the headlights reflected off the walls of the adjacent house. She listened to the benign bleating of the alarm. The miniature crash of his keys on the counter. Anne froze, her eyes landing on everything she had touched.

He called her name, and she went downstairs. He looked both windblown and deflated.

Anne asked, "Where did you take her?"

"Skating," he grumbled. He wiped his hand over his face as if he'd been worn down over several lifetimes by scores of different females.

She followed him into the living room.

"Sit," he ordered. He slopped some wine into a glass and thrust it into her hand. She slid into position on the couch. He'd been drinking before Anne's arrival. Now they were drinking together. Again. Because that's what they did. They drank because it filled the spaces left by the things they could never do.

Then the phone rang, and his whole body stiffened. He groaned and looked at the clock.

"Don't answer it," she said. They looked at each other while the ringing went on, until finally it stopped. "I'm tired," Anne said like a penitent. Her head fell back against the couch. "So tired."

Dr. Breen made an annoyed grunt. He went to the mantel and turned on the fireplace. The fake log sprang to life in perfect, efficient blue flame.

Everything was sinking. Slowly, luxuriously, like a lumbering cruise ship. She could have dinner and change clothes in the time it took for the hull to fill with water. Everything piling up against the gunwales in a heaped mess before the whole ruined thing went under. She inhaled deeply while her heart banged glumly on. "I lied to you," she said. "A lot."

He scratched his chin and looked around the room. So did Anne. She groped around with her eyes for something pleasant to latch on to. But everything looked phony. The plants, the glass, the Euro-mags. Designed, put there. Camouflage for the human mess underneath.

She grinned. It was something she did at exactly the wrong times.

The phone began to ring again. Again he didn't move to answer it. When she thought she couldn't hack another inertial second, he came at her and straddled her legs, his knees sinking down into the leather cushions with a moan. He was mountainous. He laced his hands around her neck. She felt each of his fingers, his thumbs against her Adam's apple. He tightened his grip. It was marvellous, in a way. Because there was nothing left for her to do. Everything was already happening. Her eyes throbbed with blood. He squeezed and her cheeks began to flame and her throat felt like it was full of metal. He squeezed deliciously. Her lungs complained but only a little. A blackening arose at the peripheries of her vision, a funnel of light with his face at the end of it. Then the room shrank. The scene became distant. She became a dot reflected in his eyes. *Oh, come on*, she kept thinking. People had cheated for a million years. All of this for nothing.

Then the ringing stopped. He let go. The light came back to her in tingles and stars.

He got up and slunk back to the fireplace. He filled his glass again and gargled it back.

"Do you want another?" he asked.

"No," she croaked, rubbing her throat, unsure what he meant.

Anne coughed and struggled up off the couch. She recomposed her hair. The room took on a dreamy, inconsequential glow. When she left he didn't follow. She went looking for her coat, feeling her way down white tunnels of hallway, before realizing she had never removed it, her jacket with its third button missing. She left his house and took the long way home, walking tall, as if she were invincible.

In the morning Anne showered and dressed, put on lipstick and perfume and bustled out to her exam in a big rush with her big umbrella that parted the tide of walkers. She arrived at a cavernous old drill hall at the far reaches of the campus. Dr. Breen was nowhere in sight.

Mighty lamps hung by long cables from the ceiling, casting light that was grainy and penal with dozens of overlapping shadows. Ceiling fans whirred lazily, stirring the inadequate heat. Anne went with her fellow students – books across their chests, pens tapping on the covers – into a vast grid of desks, each of them taped with a name. She swam out in search of her own.

Hers was in the first row directly facing a lectern. The seats filled quickly around her. She looked left and right and found herself hemmed in by Dr. Breen's female admirers. They weren't so impressive up close. They wore scuffed shoes. They had pimples under their makeup. Big earrings dangling from stretched earlobes.

She looked down at her blank exam booklet, at the pencilled student jottings left behind on the desk. A microphone crackled, and the hall fell silent. Someone told them to begin, and she was submerged in the noise of rustling paper. Her hand trembled. She flipped the exam over and read: *Identify ethical issues in the following scenarios while highlighting the potential legal implications of each . . .*

Anne looked up and caught sight of Dr. Breen burning down the aisle, brow furrowed, his mood billowing out behind him in an invisible cloud. His eyes landed on Anne like a smack. Her gaze fell back down to the test. She heard his briefcase crash down on the lectern. It clicked open, first one latch, then the other.

Dr. Breen came near, but she didn't look up. She smelled him just before glimpsing his trousers and shoes. He pressed a finger, one long index finger, onto the corner of her desk as he passed. He tapped it once and kept on walking.

Her pen hovered at the top of her paper. Her mind froze. She could think of nothing to write in answer to his questions.

The second time he passed, she let her eyes plead. In answer to this entreaty he slid a manila envelope onto the very corner of her desk. It teetered and skidded to the floor. She pinned it under her foot.

Time was called, and she had only just begun to write. Her hand ached with the downloading of words, spumes of them, sorry and cathartic. Anne heard sighs. Chairs scraped around on the floor. A hand came and whisked away her indiscreet scribblings.

Anne tore into her envelope and found nothing more than the paper she'd never bothered to pick up. She flew to the last page where his red pen had failed her, weeks and weeks before. She gripped the margins of this neat packet of paper, and it crumpled in her hands. She panted. The students around her stood and fell away. She endured the minutes with Colette's air-headed mantras shouted out in her head. Dr. Breen leaned against the wall. She sat anchored to her chair, made of lead. He glared at the clock on the wall until the second-to-last student trickled out. It took a long time. Her eyes flamed with tears. Did he know what this meant? She was not a crier. She hadn't cried in years.

"Dr. Breen," she said, getting up from her desk.

But he wasn't listening. He poked around for the armholes of his jacket. He shuffled exams into his briefcase, and
the sound of paper was killing her.

She travelled back to the house like a zombie and found
Colette dumping her potion down the kitchen sink. "What
are you doing?" Anne mumbled.

Colette answered, "Giving in to biology." She squinted at
Anne through swollen eyelids. "What's wrong?" Anne held
up her hand and veered away and stumbled upstairs to bed.

She slept, plowing into it fitfully, wrestling with the
pillows. In her dreams she pawed like a dog at the foot of
a dune. Her mouth was full of dust. Her fingers touched the
hard edges of a thing she needed so desperately. A thing swallowed by cascading sand, an object she could never quite see.

She woke up in the dark to the sight of Colette, silhouet-
ted in the light from the hall.

"You were crying," said Colette.

"I was?"

Colette parked her formidable ass on the edge of the bed,
crushing the mattress, rolling Anne towards her.

"I had a nightmare," said Anne. "I failed my exam."

"Well," said Colette. "I think maybe you did."

Anne let the seconds pass, let her thoughts coalesce and
fall back together again. It was the middle of the night. She
felt she was waking up to a dream and not to the crispness of
life. She groaned and rolled over, covering her eyes with the
heels of her hands. "What am I going to do?"

Colette shrugged. She opened the blinds and pointed down at the yard. "Look," she said. It nearly glowed in the dark. "Snow." Anne did as Colette said, since there was nothing else left to do. She rolled over reluctantly and peered out her window. To the lawn in its fresh whiteness. The next best, fascinating thing.

HOMOLOGY

We are snarky the way people can be when they know each other too well – lazy about basic decency. The lineup snakes towards the check-in counter. Our flight, Bangkok via Hong Kong, is overbooked. All around us shorter, dark-haired people shuffle and talk in murmurs. Three airline agents chew the backlog down. The remaining seven counters are vacant, lights-out, closed for the season. For the last half-hour it seems we've barely moved.

"Passports," I say, presenting the flat of my palm.

"I never touched them," she replies.

"You paid the cabbie. I saw them next to your wallet."

"Nice try," she says out of the side of her mouth. She folds her arms, her jacket tightened between her forearms like fabric passing through a laundry mangle. Her attention transits to regions beyond my shoulder. I watch her pupils dilate as her gaze flickers over rolling objects, passersby. It's like watching her read, the way her eyes skid from margin to margin on a page. With books – as with people – our attention is ferocious but short. We leave them cracked open on our night tables, face down in exactly the spots where our interest wanes.

"Give me your bag," I say.

"What?"

"Let's check it, shall we?" I reach for the strap.

She twists her shoulder, inserting her body between her purse and my grasp. "What are you, the KGB?" She unzips it herself and peers inside, poking around as if she's afraid her cosmetics might get bruised. She zips it back up. "Maybe you left them at home," she says, "along with the nice side of your face." She slings her purse back onto her shoulder and flicks her hair into the face of the woman standing behind us.

I'm sweaty with nerves. Our flight boards in twenty minutes, and beyond the check-in counters, security is choked with passengers. She's not anxious enough. I'm both envious and suspicious of her cool.

"Why don't we check yours?" she suggests.

"I already did."

"Well, no passports," she sighs. "Guess we might as well go home."

I narrow my eyes at her. "Yanking my chain," I say, "will only hurt you in the end."

I hunch over my bag and dig through it, protecting the contents from her gaze. I begin to have this feeling as I pick through balled-up Kleenex, beauty products, travel-sized containers of toothpaste and lotion. I have made a grave mistake, somehow. A flush of panic blooms across my cheeks.

We aren't going to make it to our destination, and it will be all my fault.

"I gave them to you," I say.

"Uh-uh." She clucks her tongue and gives me a gloating smile.

"I swear," I say. But I'm losing my resolve even as the words leave my mouth.

Just like a magic trick, she produces our passports from the inside pocket of her jacket. She dangles them in front of me. "You didn't give them to me, and you didn't see them next to my wallet. Want to know why not? Because you left them at home in the bathroom."

It's a loathsome sort of dawning. She's going to eat up my wrongness and breathe it all over me. Before our departure, I'd rushed around with our passports in my hand, as if I didn't trust myself not to forget them. A Freudian crime, a suggestion of contrary wishes.

"Bitch," I say.

"Bitch yourself."

All around us quiet people with small children stare. We are about to make a scene. Maybe we are already making one.

We reach the front, wheeling our matching Great Dane–sized suitcases. I have a hate-on for our agent, even though nothing's her fault. She looks between us – first at her, then at me, then back to her – before averting her professional gaze. *Go ahead*, I want to say, *we're used to being gawked at by people like you.*

Somewhere at the far reaches of the terminal, our flight has already begun boarding. I'm aware of this fact like it's an emergency, like our lives depend on it. Once we check in and rid ourselves of our luggage, I point myself straight towards security, with its frosted glass doors that roll open and shut, bleeping metal detectors and frazzled-looking people shaking themselves out of their coats.

"I'm going to get a coffee," she announces. I wave my watch in front of her face. She shrugs and whirls on her heel. I'm instantly angry, as if I've been shot out of a cannon, back two decades into one of our prepubescent furies. My hand fires out as if of its own accord. I snag a chunk of her hair. Her head dips sideways. She smacks my wrist and says, "Watch it. I'll walk right out. Right through those doors. Then where will you be?"

"I'm going," I lie. "With or without you."

I pick up my carry-on. I stomp off with our boarding cards and passports flapping in hand. I don't look back to see if she's following. But I know. She'll wait until there isn't a minute to lose, when I'm at the head of the security line. Then she'll be right there, when it really counts, storming up on my tail. Because wherever I go, she goes, too.

We. Separated in age by just seven minutes. Two socks rolled up into a ball.

Our hostile situation is tentatively rectified by some bungling in the overhead bins as well as our disdain for an officious flight director. Yeah, we *know* how to board an airplane.

We wedge in against the windows and settle in. The plane takes off.

"Quit clenching," I murmur. "It's irritating."

"I'm not clenching."

"Yes, you are," I say. "I can feel it. Since when have you been afraid?"

"I don't know. I am."

"How can you be afraid? I'm not afraid."

"Don't bug me," she says. "Leave me alone."

I have it in my mind that she's faking. Building credit with melodrama, leveraging herself out of the check-in episode in the airport. "What are you afraid of exactly? That we're going to fall out of the sky? That this big, bulky sheet-metal contraption is going to spontaneously blow all its rivets and blast apart?"

"No."

"Jet failure? Fuel-tank rupture? Do we plummet out of the sky?"

She looks at me darkly.

"Terrorists," I whisper.

At the mention of this word she slaps the window shade shut and pulls her blanket up over her shoulders.

"Terrorists," I say, delighted. "Arabs with suicide bombs taped to their chests. Hairy men who want to whisper obscenities in your ear before slicing you up with X-Acto knives." I'm talking sort of loudly now, not really caring who hears me.

"Shut up," she snaps. "Don't talk to me." Her voice is warbly and thick the way it gets just before she cries. She reaches for the service beacon.

In the time it takes for the flight attendant to arrive, I decide I'm going to quit talking. She's been suitably punished in my estimation. And also, I have pushed it too far. A fear is a fear. Full-fledged scenarios with sinister middles and hor- rific endings. Essential, protective, as everyone knows. They prevent certain things from happening.

She asks, "Can I have a glass of club soda?"

Later in the flight, when she's forgiven me, when I've softened her heart with Tylenol and my magazines and a kiss on her shoulder and a few gratuitous drinks, we listen to "Sacred Sounds of the Desert." We insert the buds of our headphones into our ears. She wears the left, I take the right. The Discman spins between us like a shared artificial organ, a heart that whirs but doesn't beat.

We spread brown blankets over our laps, and we lean our heads together. We imagine that handholding is our salva- tion, the psychic cement that keeps us all in the sky, that prevents the plane from scudding apart into a thousand pieces.

At home, we share a job. We are programmers for a com- pany that makes software for remote-feed surveillance cam- eras. Who buys this stuff? We don't want to know.

In the mornings we catch the elevator to our third-floor office, a medium-sized compartment with ergonomic furni- ture and a not-bad view. We sit down at desks divided by a partition – this we don't mind, in fact we prefer it. Then we fire up our hard drives and we're off. Typing like madwomen, working up sweats, pushing coffee cups on our desks into forests of dirty dishes. At night someone comes and whisks our mess away.

Never has the CTO seen anything like us. We do the work of five people. We generate miles of code, door-stopping tombs of script. We have outstripped everyone, even the dweebs from Romania who work downstairs. They hate us. We see why. We've written so much of the code we've practically authored the whole thing. Hence the nice office, and more.

We are the company muses. Hyped, irreplaceable. We think it's hilarious. In our minds we are not much more than glorified typists. "Tomorrow we quit," we taunt, just to see what will happen.

"No, wait!" says the CTO in a lather. "Take a break. As long as you want. We'll buy you tickets to the beach."

The joke just keeps getting better. They're going to send us to Siam, the home of Chang and Eng. We laugh now, but at the end of the day I am grateful. My eyes are dried out. My brain is so tired I can't even summon my body out of the chair.

It's the Tour de Twins, a contest with many stages. All day long I hear the clacking of her keys, and I compel myself to type faster, to crank out more volume. No matter if I'm hungry or thirsty. Some days I forget to pee. When we work we sweat, gritting our teeth. Our jaws ache by noon. Pages of script zoom out of the printer. She never talks. I ask her questions over the partition, and they fly out into the void.

Some days I slack and let her get ahead, hoping she will tire. I catch myself staring out the windows at whatever's falling dully from the sky. I feel like one of those blue turds of wet lint that turn up in the bottom of the washing machine.

It's her fault I am stuck here. It's difficult to say just how.

People crawl around in the streets. Long endless streams of solitary marchers, pressing their faces into the wind, making pinched winter expressions. Stupid, lightweight trench coats. Briefcases flapping at the ends of their arms. A whole street of employees battling upwind. They make individuality look terrible.

Whenever the clouds thin, I peer out over the South China Sea. It occurs to me: We are flying over the globe, over millions of people. We could fall out of the sky and land anywhere amongst them!

We drop down into a miniature unknown world. Lush green, the brown river like a torn fruit skin. The plane plummets, and it thrills my insides. A bulb on the wingtip strobes. As the wheels touch down, my guts fold and twist with anticipation. The plane taxis to the accordioned tube of gate and the jets idle down. Passengers stand. I can't wait. I jockey with our bags and straps.

In our attack on the world I am centre-forward. She plays defence. I nudge at strangers' backs. She huddles close behind me. My whole body leaning forward, greedy for fresh air. Tumble us out of closed quarters. Get the hell out of our way!

Outside we are blasted by Bangkok, by a humidity that exceeds our wildest imaginings. We breathe the fumes of a million vehicle engines. We're unprepared for this chaos, the intensity of this equatorial sun. Still, I want to look at every glinting, hot thing. Windshields, coins on the pavement. I'll suffer the retinal burns. I want it all etched into memory. I want to roll around in it. Let me get dirty so I can go home clean.

We try to cross six lanes of honking buses and cars. She sees me leaning over the curb, about to hurl myself out into the traffic. She snatches at my wrist. Says, "No one will stop for you here."

People always tell us: you're so lucky to have each other, a best friend to be with you, no matter where you go. They are sad. They are companionless. They want to merge their assets, marry their minds. Do you really want to share everything? I ask.

Imagine: She runs through my mind like a shopper in the produce section, picking up thoughts, turning them over. She fact-checks my memory. She blows holes in my hot-air balloons. I can't even get sick on my own. Wherever I go, she's chasing. There is no place to go and quietly be, except when I am asleep. And then I worry, even as I dream, until I hear her key in the lock, the fall of her coat across a chair.

We see a man, even before we board the bus. He is bald and exceedingly pale. She makes a big clattering fuss with her suitcase, dragging it up the bus steps. I don't help her. She doesn't want me to. I know we've begun something, one of our favourite games.

We sit down on either side of him. We cross our legs. My kneecap is visible. She lets her arm fall over her thigh, baring the inside of her elbow. I see her pulse surging under the skin. It takes him less than five seconds to say hello.

He's German, a man with lost, darting eyes. On the way into the city he tells us that women are goddesses, and that we two remind him of this. He tells us he is a psychotherapist. We can see that he's lying. His sentences tremble just like his smile, and he looks at our bodies but not in our eyes. We give up on our prospects but never our playthings. We'll talk to him a little while longer.

We stare at the sides of his face, listening, unblinking, deciding he's wacko with loneliness. We watch his cheeks turn a shade of naked, genital pink. The German says he is going deep into the jungle to sleep in a hammock and eat nothing but coconuts. She gives me a look. *Perhaps he'll die of malaria.* We are cruel sometimes.

Our downtown hotel rises up to greet us, and we are on to the next thing. We uncross our legs at exactly the same moment. *Goodbye*, we say with the upturned ends of our hair, with our heels, with the backs of our turning heads. We don't believe in goddesses. We believe in each other. What need have we, Rolf, for you?

This is what I know about her: there is nothing not to know.

We saw movies in grade school about nuclear bombs. *Nucular*, said Mr. Hannigan. If it happened to us, would the school desks save us, would our handholding save us? Would we get to see each other like X-rays? Once she was slapped with a Styrofoam tennis paddle for saying *shit* in a classroom. Then I got slapped for laughing at the teacher, at the futility of trying to punish us. When she lost her virginity, I squatted in the bushes warming my hands between my knees. When I lost mine, she came down with a phantom fever. We kept a can of hairspray under the porch for cloaking cigarette smells. Our father used to say, *You live in each other's pockets.* He hated us a little, nothing he would admit to. No one could touch us, not even to teach us, back then.

Men, lovers, our would-be boyfriends. Do they know something we don't? We feel not old but belated, like opportunity has passed us by. We try to make it different, to peel ourselves apart. But we go around in circles, turning even that into a kind of race. Ectomorphs with raging metabolisms, always, it seems, hungry.

In hotel rooms we have strict unspoken rules for unpacking, no matter how long or short our stay. We must make it like home, make it our own, together and separately. We deploy arsenals of toiletries. Shared items – the hairdryer, the *Lonely Planet* – we each carry begrudgingly, divided by weight between our bags. These must appear out in the open, so no one feels cheated. When my back is turned she reorders our bottles and tubes. Later, I do the same. Our bathroom counter is like a work-in-progress, a chessboard taking shape. Who gets which bed? We flip a coin. When worst comes to worst, we split everything in half. I cut, she chooses. Our cake, our money, our shoes.

In the evening we could go out, but we don't. We have overdosed on Bangkok buzz. The motors in the street. The dank, dark humidity. It's crazy out there with sounds, smells and texture. And we have not yet acclimatized. We sit on our beds

baring our freshly waxed legs for each other, our hair slung
up in towels.

She reads a book and at the same time, over my shoulder,
a magazine. I abandon the magazine and part the pages of
our guidebook to a glossy little photo of our ultimate destination. A ragged fishing net blown right out of the ocean,
hooked on a stick in the white sand. There is a broken red
boat. I see a lone royal palm, and I imagine a place with no
people. Transparent ocean and a lip of gleaming shore. A
blank little island with room for an entire imagination.

Our trip's mission, our next contest, is an open secret.
Boyfriends, lovers, men. We're about to go out and cheat on
each other. I know, she knows. It's bad when she leaves, but
worse when she leaves with someone else. Who will hold
back when there's the desolation of being the one left out,
left behind, too late, last?

The boat skims the water, and we are infatuated with everything. The staggering meltdown of sunset, the balmy air.
The way these locals move in it, as though they have never
known cold. A tiny woman with a taut brown face and her
hair in a bun pilots the boat, throttling up and down with
her bare foot. The rest of the boat is full of Thais with bun-
dles on their laps or plastic bags at their feet. They look tired.
They take it for granted, this paradise, staring out over the
gunwales with their chins in their hands, leaning towards
their island homes.

But not us. We know when we've got it good. Tears nearly
come to our eyes, we are so overwhelmed by sensation. The

sun-dappled water frothed up by the propeller, a succulent wind in our ears. We have to hug each other to remind ourselves we are here, really here. How lucky we are after all.

We notice a white guy with a chipped front tooth. He has tanned, ropy calves. He wears flip-flops. He smokes a hand-rolled cigarette, and his exhalations fly from his mouth. The laws of aerodynamics play out in the way smoke curls around the back of his head. He gazes out at the water with a kind of familiar, appreciative calm that makes us guess he has been here before.

Of course the euphoria can't last. As we approach the island, something else overtakes us. With the onset of darkness we begin to think in anxious ways. We stop trusting the water. The tidal swell, a mild green seasickness. If the boat sunk, would there be sharks? Who would rescue whom? She smiles at me weakly, queasily, like I shouldn't even bother to ask.

The boat arrives at a long finger of jetty. The waves slap the concrete. We wrestle with our luggage while the boat rocks and grinds. The man with the broken tooth does not stop to help us. He alights and walks a confident walk to the shore. We stare at his savvy little shoulder bag, and we are jealous. We wish we were just as free.

Then he is gone and with it our ferry magic. Passengers trickle away into the darkness, and they take the electricity of arrival with them. Half of them clamber into the naked box of a pickup truck. With no sign of taxis, we follow.

We mention the name of our hotel to the driver, who, we discover, is crazy. Who drives in such a manner we can barely open our eyes for fear of dying in a ditch or a bend in the road. She leans against me as if she wants to crawl onto my lap. I can feel her holding her breath, her body tensed. I close my eyes and give in to the weight of her, because it's the way we've always been.

The hotel is not a hotel at all. It's a cluster of bamboo huts, the kind occupied by monkeys or prisoners of war. We wake the owner from a twitchy dream in a beach chair. We are speechless. He leads us grumpily by lantern-light.

Ours is a hut on bamboo stilts among the palms that fringe the beach. We stop with our hands on the door, but we find that our host has left us. We are weary and motion sick and slightly afraid to venture inside. *But the ocean* – we cheer ourselves up with this thought – *it's right here*. We step over the threshold and flip on the light.

We requested two single beds but look what we've received – bunk beds draped with mosquito netting. She looks at the arrangements and jams her fists against her hips, as if it is a personal insult, the ruination of romantic plans.

"Great," she says nastily. "Very *Year of Living Dangerously*."

We are just old enough to remember this film. We watched it together. I say testily, "That was Jakarta. This is not Jakarta."

Just like that the air is sucked right out of the room. She whirls on me, covering her ears, looking like she could rip the hut to shreds just to get at the air that's outside. "Shut up," she hisses. "Just shut up. Why do you always have to be right?"

With the whip-end of my tongue I have pestered our creature awake. Now we must coax it back into its cage. So we do what we always do. We stop talking. We stand shoulder to shoulder in the doorway and let the breeze glide over us. Our hair intermingles.

"The ocean," I say. It's dark and moonless, but we can smell it, hear it tumbling on our shore.

We slip around one another in the bathroom while obscene bugs whiz in orbits around the light bulb. We are mirror images of each other. Her lip curls down on the right, mine on the left. We have black diamonds at the edges of our irises. Mine on the right, hers on the left. We stand side by side, drawing red circles around our lips. Our faces crack into weirdly asymmetrical smiles. There is comedy to our doubleness.

We've spent months, years, gazing into each other's faces. Obsessed over blemishes, the details, the weight of imperceptible differences. When she is cold, I see the hairs stand up in the follicles. When I am nervous, she knows my tongue is as dry as a paper bag. She slides the cheese off pizza. Sleeps with the windows open. When she chews it's in a circle, like a cow. Like me. She does this. She likes that. I know everything there is to know.

Together we are traffic-stopping, but unremarkable apart. And so we always wonder: Whom do you prefer? We love men. We always have. They make fine companions and even more excellent judges.

In the guidebook we read a review of a restaurant down the beach that serves fish grilled to perfection. We decide without discussion that this is what we want. We want something else, too. It's right on the tips of our tongues.

On the way to dinner we dip into an open-air bar that throbs with techno and whirling, moth-like light. Only it's dead. Four women sit like compass points with their sexy dresses and tanned backs and their sweating drinks. We enter, and all four heads turn as if attached to a single, resentful creature. The bar has a skirt made of palm fronds. This entire corner of the world, we see, is dressed in a skirt.

We slide onto barstools. The bartender saunters towards us with a rag over his shoulder. He wears fisherman's pants and no shirt. He looks between us and licks his lips. He spreads the fingers of each hand on the wood at our elbows. "Oh, my," he says.

We know what he is thinking. Many men have thought his thoughts. He is imagining what it would be like to have sex with both of us at the same time. We don't even have to look at each other to agree we are invincible.

"I know exactly what you want," he says. He fixes us matching drinks.

We look him over. His naked chest tells us of his daytime occupations: meticulous tanning and push-ups in the sand in perpetual preparation for exactly these moments. He slides two glasses over the bar – frozen blue froths piled in martini glasses with maraschinos skewered on plastic rapiers. We bet he doesn't drink. We bet he used to like to. He is American. His name is Mick. A Maori bone hook dangles at his throat. We wonder about the traveller-girl who gave it to him.

Mick bores me. Gorgeous looks, average charm, too accustomed to being chased. I tell her with a glance that I cast him aside – just like a bag of clothes for her to rummage through. I slide him a couple of American bills. I abandon my drink and cast a commanding look in her direction.

"We're hungry," I say, swivelling off my stool. "We are going to eat fish."

"Come back later," he says.

"Maybe," she sings.

His eyes pierce with intent. He tells us, "Once you've had your fish, come back. I'll pour sweet, frosty drinks down your throats. I'll get you nice and high."

"Thank you," she says, hotly startled by the way he talks.

"No," he says. "Thank me later."

She does this next thing so slickly it feels like a pickpocketing, and after a fashion it is. She stretches towards Mick, baring her cleavage, and hooks her finger through the hole in his pendant. He leans out over the bar until their faces come close. "Give it to us," she says about his trinket. "Then we'll have to come back." He doesn't think twice. He does exactly as she wishes, for now and also for later. He takes it off and winds the cord around and around. She drops his necklace into her purse.

We leave. She walks in front. Quite abruptly I want to step on her Achilles. As soon as I think this, I find I have already done it, kicked her in the calf with the point of my shoe. I fall against her shoulder blades as if it is an accident. She doesn't even flinch. She shakes her hair and hikes her purse strap higher and goes right on leading the way.

We dust off the soles of our feet and feed the straps back into our shoes. An array of stepping stones leads up to the patio. We hop from one to the next.

A man with an English accent greets us. He is the man from the ferry with the lean body, the chipped tooth and the curling smoke. My heart leaps. He glances between us, in his gracious hurry, without a shred of fascination with our likeness. I'm intrigued by this oversight. I have a thing for the ones who couldn't care less.

I examine the width of his shoulders as he ushers us to our table. I decide what the crease on the back of his neck says about his age, and what that might mean for me. He draws out chairs at a table overlooking the beach. He leans his khaki thighs against our table and lights the candle. We lock gazes, my sister and I. *Wow*, I say with my eyes. We are on an island in the Pacific, and he is ours for the moment. I will eat slowly. I'm glad to be wearing the best thing to come out of my suitcase.

"To drink?" he asks.

"I don't know what I want." I flash him my throat. "Make me something fun."

"And?" He rubs the lighter between his palms.

"The same," she says.

He bows and retreats.

There is a hot, salty breeze. She squints into her menu, pretending, on some level, that she can't see. The feigned handicaps, the attention-getters from childhood. The things she doesn't even know she does.

Other diners huddle over flickering votives. A cluster of

gay men. A couple with two fidgety children. A woman with severe fuchsia lips and a glow-white pageboy. Her husband, in a madras shirt and gold pinky ring, budges his cutlery around on the tablecloth. I pretend to be interested in the fishing boats that hover offshore with their wing-like spreaders and their glaring klieg lights. I scan the periphery for our waiter.

My sister slaps her menu shut and squares it under the points of her elbows. I feel the sudden urge to dive into the menu, to lay claim to my dinner choice. It's because our tastes are too close. But never should we order the same thing.

He returns with a beverage gimballed in the thumb and forefinger of each hand. He does not make fun drinks. He makes tall, clear drinks cluttered by nothing but ice cubes and lime. I like him even better.

I look up at him and point down into the menu. "Is that what's good tonight?" I feel her eyes all over me, scouring.

"It's good every night," says our waiter, who I am beginning to believe is more than just a waiter. Who acts with the smooth, aloof confidence of an owner who knows exactly what he's got to offer.

"Then that's what I'll have."

"Excellent choice," he says, sliding menus out of my hands.

When he's gone, the rims of our glasses kiss across the table.

"Excellent choice," she says, with a sarcastic wink.

A pregnant Thai woman delivers our food. It sizzles on a platter.

"*Khaap khun kha*," I say, mangling the words. It's a phrase I learned from our book. The Thai cook delivers our plates, drifts away without a second glance.

"Schmoozer," sniffs my sister.

We dig around in our curry and find it vicious with spice. Our faces melt. We honk our noses in our napkins, wonder if the cook is satisfied with our pain. After a while the heat dies back on our tongues. With our forks we comb for clean grains of rice.

Our waiter returns.

"What's your name?" she asks.

"Graham," he says.

"Look, Graham," she says in a tetchy way. "I believe what we need is another drink."

"My wife," he says, removing their plates. He points his thumb at the kitchen. "She has this thing for chilies."

She looks at me with deep, ancient, smouldering satisfaction. My pride drops down on buckling legs.

I wake up in the middle of the night. I look up at the underside of her bunk. I know without checking that her bed is empty.

She returns much later. She undresses stealthily and climbs the ladder up to the top bunk. I see the bulge in the mattress, hear the squeaking of her springs, and I know. A smudge of purple dawn on the other side of our window. For somebody, somewhere else on this beach, it's about to look very romantic.

I get up and turn on the light and stomp to the bathroom

and back again. I fling myself down in my bed. The whole frame shudders. If I can't sleep, then she, too, must stay awake. Only she doesn't budge. I stand on the edge of my mattress hanging on to the edge of hers. I peer at her face in the pillow. Her mouth sags open, her breath vaporized booze. If I lit a match it would light up the room and singe me. I flick her nose with my finger. Nothing. I don't sleep for the rest of the morning. Or if I do, it passes in a fitful eye blink.

By the time we get out of bed the day is ablaze. I hear her trilling in the bathroom, a gloating sort of tune. She glides from the bathroom wearing a bikini, a sarong around her hips.

I stagger out of bed and grab her by the wrist. I sniff her hair. I bend her head back to scrutinize her neck, where there's a postage stamp–sized red mark.

"What's that?" I accuse.

"Heh," she laughs, brushing my hand away as if I am a slow and stupid bug, a male mosquito, nothing to be taken seriously. She slides behind her dark shades.

She goes out. The sun is a hot and white, like a description out of a Camus novel. The view from our porch looks like a brochure cliché. I follow her outside into a breeze that combs the palms. She's a shiver of fabric, a fringe of blowing hair, down to the edge of the beach. My heart travels out of my body towards her. A quick wish like a bullet that explodes into flowers. A heat that's only practising.

Three tanned, sinewy guys play a lopsided game of volley-ball. The server hammers the ball, and it bounces off the sand. She hops over it, grinning in a faux-shy way that lets me know she saw it coming a decade before. She laughs out loud. The white ball rolls. These men watch my sister's breasts from behind sunglasses, their oiled shoulders gleaming. One of them runs a circle around her, fetches the ball, then jogs backwards to the net. They're Australians. *Stupid men*, I think, lingering among the trees.

I slink into the shade. She charges down to water the shade of cool-mint mouthwash. Stepping over the waves, wading deeper and deeper before launching into a strong front crawl. We always know when the other is being looked at. It feels tighter than jealousy, like a thankless omniscience.

Later in the day we laze about in an open-air café. We play chess. She slaps my arm and says, "Look."

Walking down the sand, side by side, are two women in matching Bermuda shorts and sun hats of the wire-brimmed, folding variety. They have curds of white flesh on their thighs. They soldier awkwardly in the sand with their feet in white Keds. They press their hands to the back of their heads to keep their hats on in the wind.

We do what we always do when we encounter other twins. We freeze like moths on the bark of a tree. We slide on our sunglasses and slouch in ways we think make us look different. Twins. Who wants to compare notes? We are our own exotic species. We like it that way.

We swivel our heads. We see that these women are not twins at all. They are merely companions, dressed exactly alike. We watch these old dames until those frowsy, foldaway hats are light blue dots in the distance, until they disappear around the heads at the end of the beach.

The tide has gone way out. We put the chessmen away.

My sister says to me, "I get so fucking bored when it's just us."

In the afternoon a gauzy layer of cloud passes in front of the sun. The beach empties, and the island looks suddenly impoverished. We shove our heels back into our running shoes and we walk the path to the road. We are going to go to town. We are going to buy things to prove we were here.

Away from the beach the island rises in the centre into a jungly swell of land. On the road to town we don't pass a single house, and not a single car passes by. Sweat trickles from our armpits down our sides to our waistbands. We wish we'd brought a bottle of water. We pass the ferry landing, which in daylight is just a steep, short stretch of beach with old tires piled at its fringes. Where does everyone live?

We walk until we lose track of the time. The road curls, and around each bend is more roadside littered with plastic bags and snack pouches. Asian flavours: sweet with salty, soy themes instead of cheese. We walk until we are hungry.

"Let's go back," says my sister. We have drifted ten feet apart as people do on futile journeys.

"No," I reply. "We're going to get there."

Minutes after she says this, we find ourselves standing exactly where we began, back at the bushy front of our hotel.

We've come to an island that folds over on itself. An island without a heart. We look at our map with the dot that isn't a town, that signifies nothing. We trudge back to our hut, overwhelmed by sudden fatigue.

A smell of decaying marine life wafts from somewhere down the beach. "Putrid," we say angrily, as if the odour is somehow the other's fault. We slide our feet out of our shoes. We crawl under the mosquito net and collapse shoulder to shoulder in my bunk, worn out by the fruitlessness of the day.

"Where was the market?"

"You expect me to constantly amuse you?"

"You promised a crab salad."

"Fuck you, crab salad. You robbed me of my sleep."

"You call today a good time? I don't call that a good time."

"What is this new sluttitude? It astounds me."

"You're just jealous."

"Damn right. Where's *my* party?"

"You have no sense of direction."

"Neither do you. Mick's a skank."

"Beats you."

"Does he?"

We lie on our backs in the heat of the dying afternoon. We stare up at the ceiling. I picture a creature, washed up on the shore, recently shredded by a shark. The slanting, orange, disappearing light of the sun. All of this makes me angry. I groan and flop over and face the bamboo weave that wraps the wall.

We breathe in time together, eventually falling into a heavy nap, as if we have made the mistake of eating too much.

She wakes up in panicked sweat. "I hate this place," she pants. "Look at us. It's claustrophobic. It's itchy." She flies from the bed and into the shower.

I sit up in bed. I listen to the water rain down onto the ceramic.

Her scream pierces the newly arrived night. It sends a jolt up my spine. I am in the midst of smearing my fingers around in my eye sockets. Now my hands hang in the air. There is another shriek that silences the lamentations of the insects. She emerges half-wrapped in a towel with wet hair stuck to her forehead and cheeks. She sobs, "A millipede crawled out of the drain."

We zip ourselves into our most skin-baring dresses. We close the door on the hut. We will wear out the wrinkles as we walk to Graham's restaurant, which is where – if I have to drag her – we will eat.

We move in growling, tandem silence. At the other end of the beach the restaurant's fire pit blooms. As we near it, we see Graham's wife in the orange glow of coals. She pokes around with a stick. Sparks stir into the air.

The restaurant is quiet. We stand at the entrance and wait to be noticed. Graham moves around behind the bar with his head tilted contentedly back. Just the sight of him is like a shot of oxygen between us. An inch of lift under my feet.

He looks between us. "Bad day?"

He is canny. It deepens my crush. I watch her rearrange her face into a sultry and amenable expression. I wonder if I have already done the same. He seats us at exactly the same table as the previous night. He takes our orders. As quick as he was to attend to us, with the same efficiency he is gone. I want to cling on to his lapels. Let him drag me into the kitchen and throw me into the dish pit, if only to save me from her company.

We make no efforts at civilized dinnertime chitchat. Our food arrives, and we chew it in a cloud of dissatisfaction.

"They're sweet," she says.

I am instantly outraged. "Oh, please. Don't you think it's creepy?"

"What?"

"She's got to be twenty years younger than he is."

"Love is love is love."

It's a pretty, wishful thought. Oprah would approve. But what about *our* kind of love: I'd like to thread my fingers into her hair and take a bite out of her neck. *What about us?* I want to demand. What to call this dark tango? More resilient than a happy marriage. How do we begin to break up?

When the restaurant closes, it's just we three and a bottle of Thai whisky. Graham lets us hand-roll the last of his Golden Virginia into lumpy cigarettes. He tells us he met his wife in Chiang Mai. She worked a stall in the night market selling mock designer handbags. Her mother lives in Pattaya. Their baby will be an Aquarian, but I doubt any of these facts will save my sister and me from ourselves. We are more than a little bit drunk.

My sister and I never talk to the same man at once. We agree to be competitive about avoiding competitive conversations. Instead we tag-team Graham with our probing looks, undress him with our silence. Once he realizes this, the talk grinds down. He dribbles out of polite things to say. He gets up and sets himself to the first unnecessary task available, emptying ashtrays and swabbing ineffectually with a white rag.

"Do you want to go snorkelling tomorrow?" I ask.

She turns to me sharply, squints at me as she blows smoke out of the side of her mouth. "Absolutely not."

"Why not?"

"I'm afraid of the fishes."

"Since when," I accuse.

"Since forever."

I peer at her but I also follow Graham's movements in the background. He bends over tables, wiping in exactly the same fashion each time, figure-eights and a whole lot of nervous zigzags. "If we go snorkelling I'll release you from dinner so you can visit the American or whatever."

"That's not a bargain. I'll visit the American anytime I want to."

"Do you want to go or not?"

She points her chin in Graham's direction. "You only want what you want because the answer is no."

I'd like to hurt her a little bit – literally, physically. A bent-back finger, an accidental cigarette burn. The taste in my mouth is salty and metallic. It reminds me just slightly of lust.

Graham returns to us. He leans his knuckles on two corners of our table. I put my hand on top of his and look her in the eye.

"It's our birthday," I lie, for no reason at all. But as soon as the words leave my mouth I know I've sealed my fate.

He slides his hand out from under mine and gives it a brotherly pat. Then he gets up and sidles to the bar. He pulls the plug on a long string of tikki lanterns. We fall into tropical darkness. Across the table I see her cigarette end flare, glowing triumphantly.

"Well," he says.

Graham walks us to the exit. The ghost of her back disappears ahead of me in the darkness. I feel the sudden warmth and pressure of his hand on my spine. He eases me forward and down off the last stone, which has an awkward concavity to it. His touch travels from my elbow, down the hairless strip of my forearm, over my palm and finally off the tips of my fingers.

By the time I catch up to her she's made it down to the water. When I call to her she doesn't wait. She continues her pace, neither quick nor slow, back in the direction of our hut. I can see from the tilt of her shoulders that her trump has failed to satisfy. That's our law of diminishing returns. Always together, never apart.

I fall into line ten feet behind her. We march in sheets of lapping ocean. In silence – a hidden wisdom – for fear of what we might unleash.

A motorbike in the distance. The eye of light veers towards us.

On the bike are two Thai boys, barefoot like us, one behind the other on the seat. The motor sounds like an aging lawn mower. It puffs out oily fumes. They slow down to an idle and scoot along next to us, propelled forward with burps of fuel. They prod at us with their eyes.

"Okay, boys," my sister shouts. "It's time to shove off." She flicks her nails, as with water at an iron, towards the undeveloped peripheries of the beach.

The boys laugh. They take off. We are left feeling disappointed. Have we seen all there is of the men? Is this all the island has to offer?

We watch the motorbike careen down the beach then veer around in an elliptical doughnut. The bike charges back towards us. Our bodies drift together, and we are homesick, quite suddenly, for the safe simplicity of our hut. As the bike gets closer we clutch on to each other's arms, sure that this hunk of sputtering machinery will flatten us. The bike swerves at the last second, so close we feel the headlight on our skins. As it passes, sand pelts my dress like a shovel-load of shortbread crumbs. The boy in back snatches at my sister's breast.

"Did you see that?" she shrieks.

I shrug. I have no idea if we should be worried. We never had brothers. The bike loops back around. Their tire chews up the sand. On their second pass, they lift my sister's purse away from her shoulder. I can almost feel the scrape of leather. What happens next is a surprise even to me. I reach and catch the strap in my hand, without a single thought about the consequences. I know coolly, without fear, that I'd fight for this object as if it had a life. Hers, or even mine.

My body bursts into action, as if I was made for it. All the muscles in my arm jerk as the strap tautens. I begin to run, dragged in the spewing wake of the back tire. The motor groans. The hem of my dress rides up on my thighs. I look into the face of the boy with the purse in his grip. He looks both cunning and afraid. A huge gulf separates this boy and me, a distance I can't even comprehend. Fifty countries, a few oceans. I wouldn't mind seeing him caned.

The purse's clasp bends and separates. The strap burns a strip down my hands. I let go, and the bike chugs away. It's been a long time since I have run like that, and I feel as if my chest will implode.

"Wait!" I hear her shout. "Wait!" But to whom is she yelling, and why?

The isosceles wedge of headlight zips away down the beach. I puff back across the tedious stretch of silvery shore. A slide of mucus cascades down the back of my throat. I arrive back at the spot where the crisis began. I've lost my shoes in the drama and have already given up hope of recovering them.

My sister has crashed into hysterics. She points her finger at my chest. "I told you we should have gotten the hell out of here."

"Don't you care?" I pant. "What if they shot me or something?" In truth I am glad she lost her purse. It was cheap. It looked cheap. Manufactured in a sweatshop by children.

"Everything was in that purse. What are we going to do now?"

We've been robbed, and yet on other parts of the beach the party whirls on. *What are we going to do now?* I am so tired of this question's burden that grains of sand in my eyelashes feel like boulders. I'm too tired to cope, flattened by a gush of the adrenaline, grimed with perspiration and beach dust. I feel my mind float out of me and drift. To somewhere better but impossible, the usual déjà vu.

"I'm leaving," I announce. "I don't care what you do."

"You can't leave," she says. "There's no boat until tomorrow."

I could cry in frustration, but nothing will come. As if to prove something, I storm out into the water. Wading in like a literary suicide, soaking my dress in the kiddy waves.

The water stays shallow. I go quite far out, stumbling into sandbar after sandbar. By the time water hits my waist I'm half-convinced I'll swim back to the mainland just to spite her. I plunge deeper into the inky sea, lifting my arms as I go. I am up to my shoulders in blood-warm water when I hear her calling my name from the shore. I'm aware it's a drama. We can't seem to escape it. It satisfies in such an odd, compelling way.

When I turn back I see her silhouette against the lights of the huts and the discos. I am hidden in the waves. She stalks back and forth, searching for me. I listen to her calls pass through layers of emotion. Urgent to angry to desperate.

She won't come in after me, I know, due to another of her supposed phobias. She hates the water at night, the creatures that lurk where she can't see them. Tentacles and spines. Sea bugs. Jellyfish. Dark and murky bottoms. I feel a little of this, too. I stand frozen up to my chin in the water. Not daring to move for fear of all the creatures that might touch me.

I walk back down the beach in fashion ruination: dirty bare feet, the wet fabric of my dress bunching between my thighs, my underwear full of sand. I'm thirstier now than I've ever been. My desire for a bed exceeds all of the above. But sleep, I know, won't happen anytime soon. She's up, lying in wait for me. I grow nauseous with fatigue just thinking about it.

As I approach our hut I see that not a single light burns inside. I'm hopeful for a moment – a pint of my blood for crisp, clean sheets. I can't wait to close my eyes on today.

I open the door and step into a different kind of air. It's thick, like that of an attic, warm from the residual heat of the day. In the darkness I know exactly where she is. Straight ahead of me, on the opposite side of the room. I hear her breathing. From the rustling of fabric I know she's still in her dress.

I am seldom surprised by her fighting techniques, yet always shocked by the fierceness of the delivery. When she lunges, I am less ready than I think. She rams me in the chest with the heels of her hands. I travel backwards against the door, slamming it shut.

We fight soundlessly, in the dark, as we have since we were girls. I wrestle her to the ground, press her head against the floorboards, covering her nose and mouth with my hand. I sink my knee into her belly. I feel her hot breath between my fingers. It only makes me thrust down harder. For a second or so I think she'll stay this way. Bowed down.

Then she unleashes herself. Her limbs go wild. Her knees pummel my rib cage. I bump the table with my head, and the contents of a cosmetic bag scuttle in all directions. When my face is turned she hooks her nails in my ear and lays a deep scratch down the side of my neck.

I back off, let go. I sit back on my heels and touch my face. The stickiness of fresh blood enrages me. I stand up. So does she. We stand toe to toe. Our breath is hot with garlic. My hand finds a wooden hairbrush, and with a deft forehand I strike her across the face with the back of it. The sound is almost athletic, like a tennis racket thwacking a ball. She falls away from me instantly, her hand darting up to her cheek.

As foes we are perfectly matched. Our scraps are interminable. No one wins. We grind into deadlock then fall apart exhausted. We can commit whatever violence we want. We can, and we do. But now I have broken a rule. Never have we struck each other as I have just done.

She crumples onto the floor and lets out a shivery sob. "Stop," she cries. I feel the splat of a tear on my toe. "Just stop."

The words, not the tears, are my undoing. I sink down, too. I cradle her face in my elbow, her head between my breasts. I paw my hand across her head in long, heavy strokes until I have pomaded her with my finger oils and each hair seems to lie down perfectly against each adjacent strand.

We stay like this until my knees are numb, our skins aflame where we have marked each other. I lift my fingers between us and make a starfish of my hand. Her skin meets mine. Fingertip to fingertip, palm on palm. Our fingers slide down the lengths of each other and land in the fleshy crooks. We squeeze with matched intensity, the blood draining from our hands.

OPEN WATER: A BRIEF ROMANCE

A new crop of students files in from the change rooms with their swimsuits tugged this way and that.

"Get in," Colby commands. "Don't make me have to tell you twice."

Each of them slithers over the side of the pool and down into eager obedience. They stand in the water on tiptoe, hugging themselves, their shoulders shrugged up to their ears.

"Names, people," says Colby. "I want names." He'll make them shiver for a while, just so they know who's in charge.

Colby teaches people how to breathe underwater. Not just any people. Accountants, judges, MBAs. People who spend their time making buckets of money, pushing paper and underlings around, doing things that are bad for the environment. They pay a fortune just to put on scuzzy U.S. Army surplus wetsuits, to have Colby whip them around. He wears a flat-brimmed ranger hat, fake dog tags and a whistle around his neck. It's the uniform at Scuba Trooper: *Adventure diving with a kick!*

Dale, the pear-shaped Ernst & Young accountant with a short body and a long ego. Hans and Linda, the retired real estate agents. Then Pamela, Kitsilano Pam, who owns a vitamin store and takes out big photo ads of her chiselled self in the centre of the wellness directory.

In addition to his hat, Colby wears an army-issue farmer john, the neoprene hanging around his waist like a half-peeled banana skin. He strides around on the pool deck in his martial, leaning way with a clipboard against his forearm. He checks names off his roster. All but one are present.

In the midst of Colby's introductory dressing-down the door of the ladies' change room swings open. His students' heads swivel. He knows without having to look that his missing party has arrived. Her name, from the class list, is Angelina. He turns to her lazily and folds his arms. He spreads his feet wide, like a cop's.

She emerges at the mouth of the locker rooms, the far end of the pool. All Colby can discern from that distance is black and white – a spurt of black hair, a tube of white towel wrapped around a torso. She approaches, cruising along the pool edge from the shallow end to the deep end. The towel is removed en route and tossed over a shoulder. Underneath it, a bikini. A black one.

The pool is quiet except for the soft suctioning of pumps and filters. Colby scratches his chin and hears his own stubble. No one has ever worn a bikini into his class, certainly not one so saucily brief. As Angelina saunters towards them she plucks its straps like the strings of an instrument. He forgets himself with looking for several long seconds until he feels the gaze of his class on his back, hungry for disciplinary action.

"Your highness," he shouts, his voice echoing off the water and between the walls. Two black triangles linger behind his eyes. Angelina startles, hops an inch or two backwards. "Do you know what happens to late arrivals? Do you know what I do?" He feels the weight of the others behind him, leaning in and breathing, the hidden curves of their smiles, their shivers of collective delight.

She starts into a clipped little run towards them. The mincing jog, the wet deck. It's inevitable that something will go wrong. At the halfway mark her foot skids out from underneath her. It jams into the base of the lifeguard stand. He hears his class's sudden intake of breath. The air seems to flatten for a half-second, and then she lets out a supersonic shriek. As it reverberates up into the rafters she hops up and down on one foot.

"Fucking thing," she screams, whipping her towel at the offending metal edge. She overshoots and the towel lands in the pool. It takes on water, spreads out and sinks. Angelina sits down on the deck to inspect the cut. Drops of blood dot the ground.

Colby walks stiffly, clipboard in one hand, pencil in the other. He crouches next to her on the ground. "Are you all right?" he whispers, out of earshot.

She glares up at him resentfully.

The sight of her cut giddies Colby with anxiety. He stands up and shouts out to the rest of his class. He listens to himself assign a ten-minute water-treading session. They grumble amongst themselves. When no one is looking he offers Angelina his hand, which she refuses, preferring to lever herself up off the floor.

He steers Angelina to the lifeguard station. They sit facing each other in moulded plastic chairs, her foot in his lap. He cleans the wound on her baby toe – nothing, really, a nick with a skin flap attached – and wraps it extra carefully with a Band-Aid. His whistle dangles. He wears rubber gloves. He hunches over her exposed pink toes, each one fleshy and uncallused and obscene somehow, up close. His face overheats, as if he were standing too close to a fire. Angelina's heel rests mere inches from his crotch.

"I don't like you," she says.

Colby replies, "Is that so?"

Their eyes meet. Hers are grey and glinting. A sparkle rises from his belly to his face to the top of his head like a vessel filling and overflowing.

When they return to the class, she goes first, swinging her hips down the deck. She slides her index fingers under the elastic at the bottom edge of her bikini, stretches the fabric down and out across her buttocks. It lands with a soundless smack.

Fasten your seat belt, he tells himself. *This flight is about to take off.*

Colby's apartment is a square, windowless arrangement, the bottom stack of a house. He lives with Roy, an old chum from high school. Their friendship is an accident of proximity. Roy has just kept turning up, being there, which, it seems to Colby, accounts for the longevity of the friendship. The lease is Colby's, so he gets the bedroom. Roy sleeps on the couch.

Roy administers market-research polls at a grim little kiosk at Metrotown Mall. *Which beverage flavour do you prefer, grapefruit or sour apple? Please list the laundry products in use in your household and rate each in importance from least to greatest.*

Roy is also an aficionado of get-rich-quick schemes. Around the apartment the evidence is everywhere. Books with titles like *Selling from the Soul* and *Millionaire Minds.* Hundreds of steak knives in Styrofoam trays. A shrink-wrapping machine. Stacks of CD jewel cases, empty. For a time Roy even sold designer vitamins door to door. Which didn't go so well, on account of his seborrhea and smoker's teeth. The latest is Angora rabbits. He came in with a plastic kitty carrier, which Colby looked at dubiously.

"You harvest the fur," said Roy. "With this special brush. Then you sell it." He freed two rabbits onto the carpet, caught a rump in his fingertips before it squeezed under the sofa. "See this?" he asked, holding up a tuft of white fur. "This is our future."

After a time, one of the rabbits became listless and withdrawn. Just lay on its side all day, refusing to eat, its little rib cage rising and falling with each breath. Turns out one of the males was a female. They discovered it at the foot of Colby's bed nursing a litter of hot pink babies.

Bunny count this month: a dozen. They hop around the house, munching on oat straw and carrot peelings, peeing on shredded newspaper in the bathroom. Roy and Colby spend a lot of time sweeping up raisin-sized turds with a broom and a dustpan.

When Colby gets home Roy stands at the sink. "Hi, honey," he says. With a steak knife he cuts open a square of shrink-wrapped plastic containing a round of frozen meat. The packet sighs open and Roy's steak clatters into the sink.

Two rabbits sit at Colby's feet, like furry doubt-meters, their vibrating whiskers pointed at his toe. "We've got to do something about this," says Colby, shaking his head.

"Dude, these animals are worth more than pot."

"We've got to do something," he repeats.

Roy rinses the tablet of steak under the tap, then shakes off the water into the sink the way Colby's mother used to with handfuls of lettuce. Then he slides it into the microwave without a plate. "Know what your problem is, man? You don't know how to think big."

"Sexy girl in my class," Colby says later, after dinner.

"Man, you're the teacher. Assert your right," Roy replies without looking up, flipping the pages of a Wal-Mart bra and underwear insert. Roy has a way of blowing up Colby's bubbles only to burst them with a single pinprick. "Better get in there before one of those GQ jackfaces does. Then you'll really be fucked." Futility is good for their friendship. It's the glue that keeps them together.

Sometime in the middle of the week, Colby decides he will ask Angelina out on a date. As soon as he makes up his mind, the logistics bristle up. What if she never returns to his class? And where does he think he'll take her? Crappy hour at Sushi Boy? How about a hot dog outside the gates of the Playland? Colby drives a rusty white van with a metal grille separating front and back. Milk crates full of crapped-out scuba gear, bungee cords, empty scuba tanks. The kind of van driven by child abductors. Appropriately, it has soft brakes.

Colby's history with women has never been good. He's a magnet for wackos and depressives. Girls with other boyfriends, girls who wield jackknives. Girls who spin like tops. But Angelina. The long legs, the pretty skin. At night, in bed, he loops the mental tape around and around her body before tugging her away with him into sleep. During the day he imagines her fingers playing on his neck as he's driving. She steps into the shower when he's got soap in his eyes. But when he turns to her he never knows what to say. It doesn't seem to matter.

The day he met Angelina, the rent was due. Now it's a week overdue. The scenario is further complicated when Roy sinks a month's wages into the latest scheme, newly minted Iraqi dinars, the world's most volatile currency. Colby makes skimpy money teaching scuba, less than his students could ever imagine. Less, he is sure, than the boys who skim leaves from their backyard pools.

"What about the Angora?" Colby asks.

Roy says sheepishly, "I guess no one knits sweaters at this time of year."

To make up for the shortfall Roy supplies the house with a thousand sachets of Pantene Pro-V Relaxed & Natural.

Plus enough Grape Gatorade samples to get them through hangovers for the rest of their relaxed and natural lives.

Colby has never served in any branch of the military, but he looks the part, which is all that really matters. A man without a shred of superfluous flesh. Tall in stature but faintly ugly – overgrown, cartilaginous. A civilian with an ancient undersea past that's both modest and glorious, in memory if nowhere else. He's dived for abalone in the Gulf Islands, scrubbed barnacles from the hulls of Royal Vancouver yachts. Visited with sea tortoises. Shipwrecks. Fish that glow as if shot through with X-rays. He loves the ocean's ups and downs as well as its forwards and backs. Life in every direction. When he dies he hopes it's underwater. Swept away in a current, caught up in the kelp fronds with phosphorescent sea dust trailing from the back of his hand. But for now he's a Scuba Trooper. Down with the pucks at the bottom of a rented pool.

Now he sits alone. The water is still, the air sultry. The arc lights dimmed down. He scans quizzes with a red grease pen, making ticks here and there, giving things a pampered, attended-to look.

Under the quizzes, it occurs to him, is a stack of folders, organized by his students' last names. He rifles to Angelina's and spreads it open. He wipes the flat of his hand across the pages of her crinkled forms. He runs his eyes over the pages for the purposes of gathering intel.

He studies her address, the street and cross street. Angelina lives high on the side of a mountain, above the smog and the fog, with the rock stars and the car-sales moguls. Where the cops stop pedestrians who don't look like they're paid – nannies or professional dog-walkers. Colby lives below, in smog, in the pink-toned concrete flats.

The purple ink. The loopy curves. Five feet, five inches. She gets ear infections. But the worst comes later, down the page. He's left momentarily breathless, as from a quick, sharp hug, when he lands on her date of birth. He does the math backwards and forwards. Angelina is sixteen years old.

Of course, he thinks. What a surprise. His life is one giant cocktease after another. Only he's the last one to know. He looks down at his right palm. It shines with the patina of his bodily oils. It's come to this. Seduced by the wiles of a mere teenaged girl into whacking off like a pervert in the bushes. Whiffs of chlorine, sanitizing and faintly punitive.

The rest is masochistic investigation. She takes birth control pills. Birth control pills! He falls into a hacking fit, and sheaves of paper side-slip everywhere, skidding into the wet spaces between the floor tiles. He gathers the forms into a jagged pile and slaps the folder shut on top of it.

His students file in like balls in the rack of a pinball machine. In their hundred-dollar sweatpants and their designer flip-flops with towels slung around their necks. He hates them tonight. They talk amongst themselves like rich people do, as if they're connoisseurs of everything, as if ignoring certain odours in the air. But most of all he hates Angelina for arriving, last in line, in another bikini. It's red, even smaller than the first.

Colby shuffles his papers and gathers himself, hoops his whistle string over his head. "All right, dirtbags. Shut up and stand at attention!"

Immediately, they do. They peel off and line up in their Speedos along the brown lip of pool deck. They face the shallow end like penguins.

He feels devilish and sharp. "In all my time teaching people like you, I have never seen a zero on a test. In fact, I think one would have to *try* to score so low. I take that as a personal insult." He stands behind Dale, the bean counter, who has thinning hair, who tries to hide it with a ball cap. With his red pencil Colby flicks the cap off Dale's head. It lands in the water with a little *thwap*.

"No hats!" Colby barks.

"Sir, yes sir!" says Dale.

Colby continues down the line, passing behind Linda. She strains to look at him without turning her head, from the corner of her eye. He moves in towards Angelina, close to the brown curve of her back. He feels his own breath steaming out of his nostrils, hot against his upper lip. Close enough to yank the knots from her bikini strings.

"Now then," he says, "will the loser please step up?"

Silence. The undulating whir of overhead fans, a seething of blood in his limbs. He stares at the crown of Angelina's head, a dot of white scalp. She squirms away from him, her toes inching towards the water. He pushes in closer, looming, until he can feel her body heat against his folded arms. There's a mole between her shoulder blades that looks like a Cocoa Krispie. Two whorls of downy hair. A vibration in the zone between Colby's navel and his crotch, a humming like distant chainsaws.

"Fine," Angelina snaps. "It was me already."

"Thank you," he sneers. "Angelina scored the zero. So it's two hundred metres for you all."

"Right now?" asks Linda.

"Linda," he says, rubbing his temples, "I feel a bad mood coming on."

Administer as punishment what they're required to do anyway – a trick that never gets old. Before they launch out over the water into dives and giant strides, the class turns to look at Angelina. They burn her to the ground with their scowls. *Good*, he thinks. He'd like to punish her, too, but in his own special way. Right now she has no idea. And neither does he. He's a dog, teased at the end of its rope. Afraid to let himself go.

Dale kicks away first into the requisite warm-up swim. He flounders down the pool in an inefficient froth. Hans and Linda wade deeper along the sloping bottom and into reluctant front crawls. Pamela glances up at Colby and follows his sightline to Angelina. Then slick as a mink, she pushes off from the wall. Like Colby, Pamela has a body made hard by unrelenting workouts. He's careful not to look at her directly, afraid of having his eye gouged by the giant diamond on her finger. He's afraid of what they might have in common.

Angelina hangs her toes over the edge, clinging to the curved metal of the ladder.

"Get in," he says.

"I have a fever," she says.

Colby leans on his heels. "You can't swim," he says. "Can you?"

"I can. But I don't want to."

"Get in," he growls at the back of her head. The rest of his students are well into their laps. "If you don't, I'm going to push you." She turns to sneak a peek just to see if he's serious. He unfolds his arms and hardens his face.

She sits down on the pool's edge, slides in and dunks herself to the shoulders. A modicum of tension flows out of his body – it's because she's simpler to look at as a head and two shoulders. "Well?" shouts Colby over the crash of limbs. She stares, unblinking, from under her dark bangs. She looks away from him drearily, takes a big hopeless breath, then leans out into a hesitant dog paddle. She struggles in the most inefficient swimming style he has ever seen. There is no name for it, this crude stroke. It's the swim of ape-men, simply the motions of survival.

Eight excruciating lengths. By the end there are full-blown tears, shivery sobs. Angelina crabs her way out of the pool. She gets a knee on the deck, then tumbles back in. She slaps the water. Her mascara has run. The rest of the class has been finished for five minutes. They stand around gaping with their elbows cupped in their palms.

Angelina climbs the ladder. The water trails her an instant behind. At the top it collides with her body and splats onto the tiles. They exchange killing looks. Colby watches her stalk down to the change rooms. Even the sight of her bare heels makes him furious with loneliness and lack. Colby, with his muscle-corded forearms and his beat-up watch. The sight of her exit is like a chiropractic adjustment. The swinging door, a puff of relief.

"Are you always that tough?" asks Linda. "Or is *she* getting the deluxe treatment?" She looks up at him from the water in her rubber swim cap and goggles. Linda is old enough to be his mother. She sounds almost jealous.

"Did I ask you?" Colby snaps.

He has a headache. He pops two ibupros in the change room while Dale bitches about his co-workers and about the cost of the baby products his wife brings home. This drill-sergeant role takes it out of him. After every class he's lost his voice from screaming. It takes a lot of energy to be cruel.

Colby barges out through glass doors and down the stairs to the empty parking lot, where Angelina lies in wait. He hears the clickety-clack of her footsteps on pavement. He glimpses a flash of pink pants and a smear of fake fur. The purse comes at him in slow-mo, swooping around in a high, lazy arc. It hits him square above the ear before skimming over the top of his head. He sees it coming but doesn't bother to get out of the way.

He holds up his hands. "Chew your food, princess."

"Why'd you do that back there?"

"It's my job."

"Well, don't ever do your job on me again." They stand in the midst of some rampant landscaping. She's breathing like a horse. A foot shorter than he is, at least. "I don't even want to take your fucking course," she cries.

Colby backs away until he's standing in a shrub with prickled creepers that catch on his pants. He says, "Then go take a pole-dancing class instead." He realizes they are nearly shouting at each other, like lovers making a scene. He looks around. The parking lot is empty. "Okay, I'm going to bow down now. Just don't kick me or anything." Colby bends and gathers the contents of her purse. Some sort of healthful energy bar. Feminine hygiene products. A tube of lipstick. A pocket French-English dictionary. Gum. A cell phone so small he could swallow it. He stuffs everything back inside the pelt. Then he stands up and returns the purse by the strap. It's made of synthetic fur, like her coat. It reminds him of roadkill.

Angelina opens her mouth again, but Colby holds up his hand. He does not wish to learn any more about her beyond the events of the evening. He knows too much already.

"Do me a favour," says Colby. "Get a new swimsuit. Cover yourself at least." He zips his jacket up under his neck. The headache thumps with high and low notes, like the sound from a conga drum.

He walks. She trails. She says, "My parents say I need some discipline."

The mention of parents sends a shiver over his scalp and down the back of his neck, where it stays, a spasm between the shoulder blades. He approaches his van. He flings opens the passenger door and crawls to the driver's side with its jammed lock and gutted seat.

When he gets behind the wheel he's only half-surprised to see Angelina standing at the window with her hand on the glass. He sighs wearily and lowers it, wondering if he'll ever be able to roll it back up again. She hooks her fingers over the window seal and leans in to sniff the cab in a way he can only think of as longingly.

"Angelina," he asks. "What now?"

"Are you going home?"

"Yes."

"Do you live far?" she asks.

He tells her the address. He says, "Far."

"I don't." She swishes her hand in a melancholy way towards the trees at the fringes of the parking lot. "I live close by."

He puts the key in the ignition. The motor complains and struggles to turn over. He pumps the gas and rubs the dashboard with a unilateral wish to be gone. He doesn't know what's next on the tip of her tongue but he knows it wouldn't take much. At any moment she could tick them over from bad to worse, from worse to wonderful.

He flops his elbow over the window and lets it slide down between her hands. Their faces hover inches apart. "Sorry," he says. "But you can't come with me. I have spongy brakes."

He puts the van into drive. As he takes his foot off the brake the van slides out from under her hand. He drives slowly and carefully out of the parking lot, shrugging off the urge to glance back in the rearview. He knows she's there. She'll be there with bells on for the next four lessons. He knows no matter what happens, there's no more getting off scot-free. There's the unpaid rent and the collections calls and the weaselly boss. A sixteen-year-old girl breathing down into his collar.

As soon as he walks in the door, Roy intercepts him with the phone in his hand. "Dude," says Roy in a leering, amazed tone that lets Colby know it couldn't possibly be the landlord. "Message for you." He listens. It's Pamela. He dials her number, reaching her in Organics Plus.

"How did you get this number?" he asks.

"You gave it to us," she says. "At the beginning of the beginning."

He doesn't remember doing this, but he guesses it must be true.

They make small talk. Pamela is especially good at exchanging pleasantries, as if she's warming him up to make her sale. In the background he hears the scanner bleeping her groceries. She asks, "Would you like to go out sometime?"

He laughs in a dark and semi-snide way. "What about the rock?"

"Excuse me?"

"On your finger. Is it for real?"

"Oh *that*." She sighs. "It's real, all right. But I bought it for myself."

Women like Pamela scare him. A woman who buys her own engagement ring, as if she plans to marry herself. All business, all bargains, all the time. "Lemme think about it," he says, and then he hangs up, holding the phone for a time in his hand. He wonders what Pamela's hiding behind the waterproof mascara and the bleached-white smile. Anyone who'd pursue Colby so aggressively must have something desperate in mind.

He joins Roy in the living room to absorb some TV, to watch without really watching. But Roy has a new girl with him. They noodle around on the sofa. She has a ring through her bottom lip that reminds Colby of a loose-leaf binder. Chinese slippers. Tattoos like stocking seams up the back of her legs. Her name, he is told, is Ocean.

"You got rid of them?" Colby asks hopefully.

"Who?" Roy replies, somewhat skittishly.

"Our furry friends."

"Oh," says Roy, sinking back into the cushions. "They're in your room."

"I can't deal with rodents," says Ocean. She sits up against the cushions with her hands under her thighs. Colby can tell by the look on her face that she hates him already for the simple fact of his being there.

"Rabbits," corrects Roy. "Not rodents."

"Okay," sighs Ocean. Her whole body seems to roll with her eyes. "Same diff."

Colby opens his door softly. When he turns on the light he finds rabbits all over the floor, like rolls of escaped toilet paper. They sit still, noses twitching, taking little hops every now and again in no particular direction.

Colby's bedroom is furnished with a lamp, a cardboard box full of car repair manuals, wetsuits, dry suits, masks and snorkels, a surfboard gunked up with old, grey wax. A

mattress like a berg in the middle of the floor. The comforter
is a mottled brown, quilted with threads that look like fishing line. It lies tightly across the bed, tucked under a row of
flat pillows. He collapses onto it thinking of the day, the
night, Angelina. A sensation of mild but taut vexation across
his chest. An itch under the armpits. A feeling like he could
claw at the ceiling.

He wakes up in the night still in his clothes, his shoes, his
jacket. A rabbit next to him on the bed, nuzzled in the trough
between the mattress and his thigh. It stares at him with
its sniffling nose and red-rimmed eyes looking like it's just
been crying. Next, on the floor, there is some sort of rabbit
skirmish. He rolls over to witness one rabbit in the midst
of mounting another, biting into the flesh of its neck. Soft,
benign creatures. They hump violently away.

When he isn't teaching, Colby is responsible for maintaining
the equipment and filling the tanks. Besides that, a whole lot
of nothing. Scuba Trooper's cut him down to two classes a
week, for reasons that aren't immediately clear. When he visits the shop, they evade his questions. They slip around his
gaze. He wonders if it's a smell he's exuding, the aroma of
downward slide.

These days Colby and Roy watch TV with the drapes
closed, not answering the phone in avoidance of the landlord. There's a knock at the door and they dive behind the
sofa. Roy crawls across the floor and peeks out the curtains.
Then he throws himself to his feet and goes to the door. It's

the dinars, delivered straight to the door in a brown paper package by a shady-looking Slavic deliveryman.

In the mornings Colby reads the grocery-store flyers while eating giant stacks of toast basted with margarine. Bread comes cheap. Coffee does not. Neither do butter and cheese. Then he works out relentlessly. He jogs through the suburbs. He does chin-ups on a bar in the doorway, push-ups on the kitchen floor. In the afternoons he naps in his bed, Roy on the couch. White fur in their noses, on the furniture, puffing around in the corners.

With nothing to do, all his actions spread out into incremental movements. Each task slowed down to the speed of religion. He takes a can of Old Milwaukee out of the fridge. He pours beer down the inside of a glass, studies the bubbles sailing to their deaths on the surface. Boredom, he considers, is a disguised form of waiting. Perhaps even longing. What the hell is he going to do next?

Not for lack of problems to solve, his mind goes combing for trouble, straight to Angelina. He thinks of their age difference and begins to disassemble it, like a car, like something that can be taken apart, repaired and put back together again into a new, better form. Half his age, minus one. Minus one cheers him. Minus one makes everything all right.

Angelina is early, waiting for him on the bleachers.

His eyes can't find a way to register her whole, so he starts from the bottom and travels up. High-heeled sandals with soles constructed of transparent plastic. Leg warmers. A skirt so minimal it's a fringe and not a covering. A satin jacket with a half-dozen layers of shirt underneath. Aviator sunglasses. He sinks down next to her with a sigh.

She carries cookies in a foggy Ziploc bag. A peace offering or a bribe, he can't yet tell. "Try one," she says.

He takes out one of the floury wholemeal discs and looks at the top then the bottom of it. He takes a bite, staring at her expectant face. It breaks off at his lip. He chews a mouthful of sandy crumbs. "Tasty," he says.

"They're vegan."

"What?"

"No eggs, no dairy."

"Mm." Colby nods. "Delicious."

"And sugar free."

"So you don't eat meat." Something about this offends him. It feels like a departure, a trek across a great cultural divide. She leaves him behind in the land of the craven carnivores.

"No dead animals ever touch my body."

"Pepperoni hidden between the cheese and the crust? A strip of bacon when nobody's looking?" Her vegetarianism only highlights his dirtiness.

"Never."

"That goop on your lips. Something must have died in the production of that lipstick." Why is he saying these things? Colby's gaze travels from the fabric of his shorts to his naked thigh and back again to his shorts. He feels her staring at his shoulder. He stuffs his mouth with the remaining crescent moon. He chews it into a resistant paste, struggles to get it down. He catches whiffs of her gum. Moist cinnamon breath travels down the length of his arm.

Angelina looks down at his left knee, which begins to vibrate with the staccato tapping of his heel. "Do you have a girlfriend?" she wants to know.

"Yes," says Colby. This lie seems to wound her, but only topically so. It seems they both know they're playing a game, one in which the words don't matter.

"Is she pretty?"

He glances down at his own chest where the left pectoral muscle throbs. He feels fine droplets spouting out of his pores. He worries in a sudden, preparatory way about the smell of his breath, about his various fluids and fragrances. It's a feeling he gets, like saliva before an upchuck. Signs before all surprises.

A kiss, both shocking and expected. Her lips land as high as they can reach, at the corner of his bottom lip. No probing tongue, no knocking of teeth. No lustful press of chest upon breast. Just a kiss. Just this once. The way a niece might kiss an uncle – if she really felt like pushing it.

A hot film of sweat between his skin and his clothes. A gush of blood to his groin. Doors open. Their heads jolt instantly apart. Colby leaps away from her as if stung by a hornet. Students meander in. He looks up to the skylights and thanks the black-velvety heavens with their dull little pinprick of starlight. For the delays, the interruptions, the small movements towards inevitable disaster. He parcels up the cookies and lays the bag in the space between their thighs. "Thank you," he stammers. "Thanks."

He clutches the frame of the whiteboard, marker poised in hand, only to forget the gist of his lesson plan. He serves up his mnemonic devices in undeviating monotone. Without shouts or commands or insulting adornments. "What is the cause of decompression sickness, Hans?" Hans stares at reflections in the window until Linda spears him in the side with her elbow. Hans, Colby recognizes, is baffled, too. It's the missing mission. It's the lazy life. The blank stare into the middle distance.

They review the dive tables. He wonders if anyone knows, if the signs are emblazoned all over his face. He can't even look at Angelina. Listening, or half listening, her lanky body spreading out, stomach down, on the floor. As if nothing has happened, a soft skeleton, a juvenile specimen that's not yet learned to contain itself.

Tonight he's lost his verve for acting like a commando, for meanness as a scintillating shtick. His hands shake. He feels loose jointed and transparent, his innards visible to every-one.

He demonstrates the fit of a regulator to a tank nozzle. Pamela makes a show of misaligning her flange and nozzle. She opens the valve and a blast of high-pressure air escapes. He bustles over and corrects the mistake, which he realizes abruptly was not one. Pamela's arm grazes his and rests there. He looks down. His arm is beefy, fuzzed with light hair. Pamela's is sinewy and brown with the strange uniformity of an airbrush tan. It reminds him of a rawhide chew. Colby moves his arm away and twists open her tank valve. As air sighs out through her regulator, the hoses grow lightly turgid. This pleases Pam. She smiles. He looks into her face where the eyes are the blue of a lonely, wide-open sky.

In this moment of preoccupation, Hans has drifted away to the far end of the pool. Colby sees him from the corner of his eye, climbing the rungs of the diving board ladder. Nothing that would have passed even two weeks ago. The sudden stupidity of rules.

Dale has slipped away, too, following Hans's lead. He paws through the bins for the choicest gear and comes back wearing a mask and fins, a snorkel dangling under his chin.

"Can't we do it?" asks Dale. Dale's emphasis on the words *do it* leave Colby cold, paralyzed on the spot. "You know, how long do we have to wait?"

"First things first," Colby replies. But his words are exploded by a deep, echoing gong. Hans launches himself off the diving board and lands with a splat in the deep end.

After class, Pamela unzips herself from her wetsuit and into her post-lesson fleece. She sits down outside the locker rooms to wait for Colby in a vaguely girlfriendly fashion. Reluctantly he settles down next to her. She lays a hand on his shoulder and asks, "Would you like to come over for some honeybush tea?"

Pamela is a model Trooper. She does her homework, and in addition, supplementary reading from a list of her own creation. She has a way of standing in unwavering allegiance, behind Colby on the pool deck and to the side, like an aide. There's nothing she's done wrong, and yet there's nothing about her that's right.

"Pamela," he says with a sigh. "You're a really great girl." Though she isn't a girl at all but something grown-up and expectant and yet tainted by disappointment. Something altogether different from a girl.

"But?" she asks.

Things fall. His clipboard tumbles out of his hands and clatters to the floor. The sound is disastrously inappropriate, almost celebratory, like cymbals. Pamela stands up. The towel peels away from her lap and drops to her feet. She stoops to pick it up. By the time she is upright again her face has melted. The tears roll. Colby puts his arms awkwardly around her shoulders and without thinking glances down at his watch.

He listens to her cry for precisely one minute. Then, just like that, she stops. She pushes off from Colby's chest and steps away. Another minute passes, and the impenetrable white smile is back.

"Don't worry," she assures him in between deep breaths. "I'm totally, one hundred per cent fine."

Colby finds an envelope wedged between the door and the seal. A letter, nicely typed and professionally worded. The second of its kind to arrive on their doorstep since the non-payment of the rent. He never realized eviction notices could seem so polite, so word-processed and inconsequential. He rubs his forehead and looks at the bug carcasses in their cobweb cocoons and for the first time the thought occurs to him: Why bail the boat when it's easier to sink? And if it's easier to sink, why not dive? Wake up at the bottom where the light doesn't penetrate and everything he does is invisible.

Colby enters his home and heads straight for the bathroom, where, behind the toilet, the rabbits have produced another litter. He storms out into the living room. "Roy," he announces, aiming down the length of the eviction letter in his hand. "If we've got to go, you're going first. And you're taking these fucking rabbits with you."

Roy gets up off the couch and retreats into the kitchen, as if he's not heard and, at the same time, been expecting this news. He rummages in the cupboard and produces a half-consumed bag of Smartfood. The foil crinkles as he dips his fingers inside. When he puts his hand to his mouth, a snow of white kernels flutters down to the floor.

The next day – not without a lot of thinking and stalling and measuring of the pros and cons – Colby drags himself into the dive shop to request an advance on his paycheque. He finds his boss reconciling Visa slips behind the counter. He wears his Scuba Trooper T-shirt tucked severely into the waistband of severely ironed Dockers.

"Colby," says the boss, "the answer is no." He is one of those people who repeats Colby's name, a habit that makes him leery. "I've had some complaints from the students." He drums his fingers on the counter, which is a sheet of Plexiglas covering a photo montage. One of the snapshots features the boss with Bruce Willis. They stand in their scuba gear on a duck board surrounded by a flat plain of open ocean. Arms around one another, thumbs up. "I hear you've been soft, even lenient. Exorbitant praise, that sort of thing."

"Who?" Colby asks.

"Not at liberty to discuss. Got an email petition from the people in your Thursday."

"That's why you cut me down to two a week?"

The boss sighs and scratches the top of his head. "Colby, let me be frank. That van. Get the muffler fixed, for god's sake. We can hear you coming a mile away, even when the compressor's going. And look at those shorts you're wearing. Where did you get them? The lost and found? I, personally, do not give a rat's apple what you wear. Heck, I'd like to have the luxury of looking that unprofessional. But I can't. I've got to look like a winner. You should want to look like one, too."

Colby skulks out of the shop, wishing he could slam the sighing hydraulic door. He climbs into his van, shuts its door with a rusty screech, then guns the motor until it backfires.

Dale plays hockey on the weekends and takes Colby's dive class on Tuesday nights. In the locker room Dale solicits details from Colby's personal life, as if they are buddies, as if the locker room bonds them as men. "Pamela," says Dale. "She wants to eat you." He likes to razz Colby about his unseen bachelor adventures, his imagined ladykilling prowess. Dale, a married man, exhibits a superior kind of inferiority. He wants to know about Colby's qualifications, what gives Colby the right to alpha his beta.

Out on deck, a grand clutter of scuba equipment spreads

out like entrails all over the floor. His students plunge into the task of assembly. Angelina appears. She wears a T-shirt. It hangs to the middle of her thighs and is printed across the chest with a huge black font that reads: FCUK. He works his eyes over the letters. How cleverly teenaged, this eye trick. Steeling herself with profanity. Pamela works it the opposite way, disguising her dirt in cleanliness, spirulina and fat-free yogurt.

If glances were threads the room would be webbed. Wherever Colby goes in the course of his instruction, Angelina tracks him with her eyes. As much as he tries to avoid it, his gaze swerves to meet hers, like a car into oncoming headlights. Pamela looks on, omnisciently. The rest of the class, they skid over Angelina, who shifts around by the lifeguard stand, awkward and unclaimed. They look accusingly at Colby. Who wants a buddy who can barely swim, who's the hard honcho's soft favourite?

"Pamela," he says, "you take Angelina." He's not precisely sure why he joins them together. Perhaps as a kind of defence.

Pamela accepts the task with strange, outrageous enthusiasm. Then she whips her hair back into a tight ponytail and snaps an elastic in place. Angelina wanders meekly in Pamela's direction, as if to a beheading. As Colby suits up he overhears Pamela skewering Angelina with niceness. She helps Angelina, T-shirt and all, shoulder her way into her wetsuit, a worn-out pelt with a rental number written on the sleeve.

When the time comes, he points at the water's undulating surface. "Duck dives, people. Do your buddy checks. Meet me in the shallow end after your underwater swim."

He falls into the water and plummets headfirst to the bottom where the pool tiles gleam under the lights. He breathes deeply. Bubbles slide up his face. Water penetrates his hair and seeps against his scalp. It trickles into his wetsuit. Cold, and then warming. Weightlessness. He is swallowed by a feeling of deep, serene calm. He'd rather hang out here, in the inhospitable margin, until his tank runs out. But before long his students have plunged and the water is full of bodies. He can hear the wheezing-in and the tumbling-out breath whichever way he turns. Splashes, chaos, a jambalaya of underwater sounds.

He swims along the bottom and surfaces in the shallows. Only Angelina remains on deck. She climbs down the ladder with her fins in her hand. She drops in, bum first, then wades out to the middle. As she nears him he sees she has done it all wrong. Tentacles of equipment float around her.

She lifts her arms for him and he begins his adjustments, unclipping her buckles, unzipping Velcro.

"Do you see what I'm doing?" he asks.

"Don't feed me to Pamela," she murmurs. "She's a hyena."

"Good," says Colby. "Now you know the feeling."

Angelina sighs. She looks all around. Up at the ceiling where various blue and red banners announce who won what swimming championship and when. At the giant time clock with its four coloured hands. The fickle fixations of a wandering mind.

"Look at me," says Colby, looking down at the top of her head. With an expert's doting he tugs down on her straps. He stuffs her gauges and hoses into the appropriate pockets. He clips her down. He fastens her tight. "Do you think you will remember?" Later, when she's older, yoked around the neck by a cashmere sweater, married to a Dale, will she remember a man named Colby at all?

They are no longer alone. Pamela has surfaced at his side, along with the others. They gather around Colby in a semi-circle.

"Great job, people," he says to the class. Their chins drip. "I'm not really sure about what to do next. Let's just go down and hang for a bit. I'm sure we'll think of something." They gaze at him through the windows of their masks as if he is a curious underwater specimen, something they've never witnessed before.

He makes a zero of his thumb and forefinger. They go down, each with a buddy. He is left on the surface with Angelina and Pamela, who engage each other in a competition of glitches. Angelina catches her hair in her mask strap, but is trumped by Pam, who embeds her earring in Velcro, just so Colby will have to untangle her.

"What are you doing after class?" Pamela asks as he's working on her earlobe.

He says, "I was thinking of throwing myself out into traffic."

Pamela laughs but he doesn't. He lets go of her sterling silver hook. She adds, "A few of us are going out for a drink afterwards. You should come." Her eyes skip along the water to Angelina, who has never before looked so young, so beneath the age of majority. Pamela seems by contrast about a thousand years old, an expert, a hardened competitor with broken harpoons in her flanks. Angelina lowers her mask into place.

Okay, he signs to them. *Down*. Angelina's eyes brim with incomprehensible dread. She takes a big nervous breath, then wiggles her regulator past her lips. Seconds after they submerge, Angelina screws her eyes shut and latches her claws into the crook of his elbow. Nails dig into his flesh. He pinches an inch of her thigh between his thumb and forefinger and gives it a hard twist. Still no bubbles stream out of her regulator. She shoots to the surface and Colby follows. Their masks squeak down their faces.

Colby looks around. They are alone, up to their chins in the water. "Don't hold your breath," he snaps. It's the first time he's barked in weeks. "If you go down deep it'll expand in your lungs and blow your bronchioles open like popcorn."

Tears swell. "I can't do this," says Angelina. She wades to the side of the pool, casting off equipment as she goes. It floats behind her in a funereal trail of black rubber and plastic. Colby slaps the water. He's had it with the teases, the feigned failures and the helplessness. He's got grooves like little sickles on his forearms.

Beside him, Pamela surfaces. She stands up in the air like a shining survivor, her face full of victorious concern.

When they've cleared the decks, Pamela corners him underneath the leaves of a giant rubber plant. "Come on," she pleads, punching him in the arm.

"I don't think so," says Colby.

"Just one drink. And then I'll never bug you again."

Colby can guess that the converse is also true – if he

doesn't go along, she'll pester him forever. "One drink, and one drink only," he warns her. He'll treat it as an inoculation – if he says yes to Pamela, perhaps he'll learn how to say no to other things.

In the parking lot she decides they will go in her car, a BMW Z4 Roadster. The seats are ergonomically contoured, low and reclined. He stretches his legs out and his shins disappear under the dash.

He's hardly surprised when there are no others. Just him and Pam at high, uncomfortable stools and a table no bigger than a large pizza. TVs beam down at them from every direction. Pamela seems to know the bar's owner. They've barely sat down when a waiter arrives with a tray held aloft and two pink-toned martinis.

Colby is anxious, the kind of nerves that come before uncomfortable procedures – dentists, rubber-gloved examinations. He tosses his drink back in three swallows and another appears before him as if by magic. Pamela talks. He avoids her gaze, listening without really listening. The air between them is logy with tension. Pamela seems not to notice. It's because she's anxious, too – for different reasons. She has spent a long time, he can tell, blow-drying and applying cosmetics in the locker room back at the pool.

A platter of seafood arrives like a kind of relief, giving him something mechanical to do with his hands, flesh to tear out of shells with a tiny pitchfork. A lone drink arrives, even bigger, it appears, than the first two.

Pamela pushes the glass by the stem across the table. "Have another," she says.

He feels her wresting control of the evening, shimmying it out from underneath him, inch by inch.

She settles her hand on top of his thigh. As her hand warms his jeans she asks, "Fox or rabbit?"

Colby thinks for a moment and then says, "Goat."

"Fox to fox?" she says, giving his thigh a hard squeeze. "You don't fool me. Don't think I don't see what you're up to."

Guilt twinkles distantly all over his body, like a sunset on a faraway lake. He slides himself off the stool, free from Pamela's hand, and lets his feet take him away to the men's, where he searches his own face in the mirror. He washes his hands of garlic butter, once and then twice, as if cleaning up after a dirty job, or preparing for a surgical one. He stretches out the procedure of drying his hands while staring at a Viagra ad next to the condom machine. A goateed dude in a wheelchair smiles down on him with a stupid leer, rubbing his head with a towel. He'd like to punch that guy and the condom machine as well. The caption reads: *I did it my way*.

When he returns to the table Pamela sits with her legs crossed and her purse on her lap and her arms crossed over the purse. The bill has arrived. She scrapes it towards her chest and narrows her eyes at him.

Enormous martinis, an empty stomach. A gut full of alcoholic vapours. He wonders how much money it would take to get him to sleep with Pamela and if she has already considered this. She's plotted everything, including his inebriation – now she must drive him home.

In the car they listen to some terrible crooning music. Colby zips down his window and the car fills with hostile wind. He feels himself withering, his hand on the door lever, ready at every red light to stop, drop and roll. But he stays buckled in. It's the way she shifts gears and hums along with the tune. The way she drives too fast and too well.

He navigates them deep into stuccoed, tree-lined suburbia, closer to his tentative home. He stops her at a random house several blocks away from his own.

"Well," she says. "I had a really nice night. Let's do this again sometime." Their goodbye is a skidmark, a streak of watermelon-scented lipstick across his cheek and ear.

He slouches towards his apartment, down the concrete strip, an unlit tunnel. Before he can rasp the key into the lock, the door falls open. He steps through and flicks on the light. "Ah, shit," he says with a sigh.

Roy is gone. The apartment turned over so that he'd think he'd been burglarized if there was anything at all worth stealing. Gaps where Roy's stuff used to live, like a mouth with missing teeth. He's taken all of his belongings, the bottles of booze on the fridge, the books, the steak knives, the Nintendo and the TV. But not the rabbits. The rabbits sit scattered all across the room, chewing on the carpet and twitching their whiskers like nothing has changed at all. And in the middle of it all, folded into the corner of the couch like an origami swan, is Angelina.

She startles him so deeply he claws his hand over his heart and sinks to one knee, burying his knuckles in the carpet like an old, crippled man. He croaks, "What the hell are you doing here?"

"The door was unlocked." A white rabbit cradled in the crook of her elbow. She dips her nose in the fur of its back, as if she could learn something from its smell.

He gets to his feet. "Does anyone know you're here?"

"No."

"Okay," he breathes. "All right." His eyes jump about the room. He presses down on the air as if he could settle it with his palms.

He backs out of the room and penetrates the rest of the apartment, probing for evidence of Roy. Finding nothing, he steers himself to the kitchen, where he leans his knuckles against the cupboards and wipes a hand down his face. He listens to the sounds of distant traffic like snowplows in another city, another tier of his memory. Plans, strategies – his thoughts are runny, they slime into the corners of his mind. Until the ivy creeps up the wallpaper. The cupboards start to tip in towards his head. He looks down at his watch. He undoes the strap slowly and methodically, tightening before loosening, removing the peg from the hole. He sets it on the counter with utmost care, parallel to the edge of the dish rack. His mouth begins to water. He marches back into the living room as if into battle, into lovely and glorious doom.

Angelina rises from the couch and stands underneath him, a small tree under a bigger one. She's got tired, purple circles under her eyes. She says, "You've got rabbits all over your house," as if it is evidence of his insanity, proof there's nothing wrong with her presence in the midst of it. He knows right then that they'll never talk about their age difference. The fact of her sixteenness is a stop sign in the unfathomable distance, a red dot rising inconsequentially out of the horizon.

They don't so much embrace as collide. His long arms go around her almost twice. He lifts her out of her shoes. Her breasts compress against his chest. His chin goes down against her collarbone. The skin in this crook smells like pool chlorine and dryer sheets. Next to his, her pelvis yields.

They dispense with polite kissing. It isn't a struggle or an act of ravishment, but a simple trick of letting go. She slithers her tongue into his mouth, her fingers underneath his clothes. They are astonishingly expert, these tiny, nimble hands. He carries her to the bedroom where clothes are shed like peelings, no one stopping to note the texture or colours of fabric. Vegetarian no more, hungry to get underneath.

They do what they do in a quick, blinded blur. It is a moment of shimmering sensation, complete and perfect, passing far too quickly through his body. He feels himself swelling, as if his body is expanding to fill up the room. And then it is over, done with a shudder.

They lie next to one another in Colby's bed like parallel stripes. Wet between the legs and panting long after Colby pulls the string on the light. In the dark she asks, "Can I stay?"

"Sure," says Colby, unaware of his words. "Of course." He's tired. So tired. He hears the sound of his eyelids clicking shut. She nudges herself against his unaccustomed body, a spoon against a knife.

Colby wakes with a start. He pans around the room in a vague, sleepy panic. Next to him, the bed is empty, a crumple of sheets and blankets. From the slant of the sun he guesses it must be midday. Ancient-looking light penetrates the blinds. He listens for sounds in the house. Then, in a single motion, he flings the covers back and throws himself upright.

He creeps naked into the living room, where he finds Angelina on the couch wearing one of his dirty T-shirts, her slim shoulder poking out from the neck hole. She dips a spoon into his tub of Kozy Shack rice pudding and lifts it into her mouth. The back of her head bristles like a boot brush. She looks over her shoulder and flicks him a shy, tentative smile. It occurs to him now what she meant by *stay*. Something altogether more doggy and devoted than what he had in mind.

He returns to his room, closes the door and yanks on yesterday's clothes in a curious, subdued hurry. As his feet find their way into the legs of his pants, his eyes graze every object and surface, every item of his possession. By the time he gets his socks on, his hands are cold with anxiety, his back hot with the need for escape.

He returns to her in the living room, feeding his arms into the sleeves of his shirt. The room is a carpeted blur. He moves, without stopping, towards the door. Angelina scrabbles to her knees on the cushions. With one hand she grips the arm of the couch. With the other she grasps at his leg. But he's gliding too fast, swerving, stirring up a breeze as he goes. He says as he travels, "Stay as long as you want. Have some toast. Just lock the door when you go." But his voice is hoarse, barely a whisper.

He flies from the house with dried drool on his cheek, his shirttails flapping out behind. He ties his laces on the welcome mat, fingers trembling, praying his prayers that she'll be gone by the time he returns.

The air is quiet and windless and dusty with pollen. The sun shines hotly, as if to punish him. Lawn mowers hum in the distance. He feels like a bank robber, electric and alive, stepping out into the daylight after the deadened smell of the vault. Surrounded by an infinity of small things changing and perishing. The sound is terrible. Grass surging out of the ground, leaves tearing out of their buds. Laundry laughs at him from the clotheslines. Whitely ablaze, too bright to look at, even from the corner of his eye.

ISLAND OF FLOWERS

EDUCATION DELUXE

Each year her father attends medical conventions in the tropics with legitimizing titles like "Human Underwater Biology" – as if there are studies and research. He jokes like he's getting away with something. Write-offs. Scuba diving. Murder.

They, the family, skip all over the Caribbean Sea. Jamaica. Haiti. The Dominican Republic. Her mother points at a new page in the atlas, pretending this next holiday will be in some capacity an educational visit, and not strictly recreation, which is exactly what it is. "See?" Each time they go away they get closer and closer to the equator. Her mother is a head librarian. Smart about some things and stupid about others.

The girl's name is Sal. Her father is a doctor. Not just any doctor, but a *surgeon*. He takes painstaking, roundabout care to drive home the distinction with his daughter, with anyone, with strangers if the craving arises. With the women who frequent big high-rise resorts that tower and glint in the sun.

On vacation, her father always gravitates towards these types. Women who travel solo, or in pairs. Who wear crocheted bikinis and lipstick into the ocean. They have flat, tanned stomachs. Their eyes rove everywhere, as if they are looking for something they've put down and lost. Her father drinks beer at the bar with them. Or plays backgammon in the lounge. They seem taken, even fooled by him, which is odd, because everything he does in public seems to Sal peculiar and embarrassing. He whistles and sings pop songs out of tune. The way he speaks to other men, loud and too close, makes them square up and bristle. Other fathers have beards and pipes. They wear cotton and wool and only one ring. Hers is a foreigner and unafraid of ostentation. He puts the money where it shows: cars and silk and gold. Some days he looks like a pimp.

Other parents seem aligned, alike, allied. Not hers. Her mother, by comparison to her father's female companions, is relaxed and blown-out, with more and less to hide. She consumes fat novel after fat novel in folding chairs on the beach. Each day she makes a point of choosing a different chair with a different view of the ocean. She wears a sun hat and big, round sunglasses. Everything about her has gone out of fashion. She was born in a poor European country where everyone burns easily but no one ever thinks to wear sunblock. By the end of their vacations her nose and shoulders are crisped.

THEY MARCH ON WITH
THE BUSINESS OF LIFE

Still, they are just like a million families.

At home Sal's mother uses *piggy* as a verb: "If I clean up your room, you just piggy it up." Father and daughter are disastrously messy, it's true, a trait her mother says has been genetically handed down between them. Her mother believes in genetics because it's easier than acknowledging that people do what they do for reasons. Slobbery, for instance, is an excellent form of protest. Sal and her father hate the way she nags and manipulates. The ways she acts like everything is *hers*.

Her parents talk of repaving the driveway, which is more humped and cracked each spring. They seldom fight, but her mother's words are caustic with sarcasm and subtext. Who cleans the eavestroughs? Who drives Sal to school? Her mother has engineered their happiness single-handedly. Like all good propaganda, this is partially true. Slowly, she has rendered the house efficient, sealed tight, hot with forced air.

When there is a fight, it looks like this: At seven in the morning, the hour of groggy thoughts and hastened departures, Sal's father is unusually bright and insouciant. Her mother stands at the counter, slapping together ham-and-mustard sandwiches. He squeezes her bottom with both hands. She whirls. It's the purplish, midwinter moment before the sun has come up. "Do you know what I'm going to do?" he asks. She eyes him warily, the butter knife still in her hand. He trots out his *fait accompli* vacation plans. He says he's going to Martinique.

Sal sits at the breakfast table. She reads the little fable on the back of the cereal box, delving deep inside the story with its industrious Lilliputians in Quaker hats and buckled shoes who have crafted by hand each wheatlet she puts into her mouth.

"I don't want to go to Martinique," her mother complains.

"Not to worry," he says. Sal's mother isn't going at all.

"What?" Her mother goes apoplectic and white.

The cereal-box story is so quickly consumed. Sal moves on to the side panels, the list of ingredients and the nutritional info where most of the vitamins are derived from the milk. Reading will be like this for the rest of her life – diversion that doesn't quite follow through on its promises.

Martinique will be a business trip. A solo trip. A quick in and out. Something thinly to do with his practice.

"Bullshit," says her mother. With her accent, it comes out sounding unconvincing, like *boolsheet.*

Boolsheet or not, it doesn't change the fact that he's going. He flaps his arms into his big czarish coat and flips up the shearling collar. He takes his leather gloves out of the pockets, slaps them against his palm, then wiggles his fingers inside. Never hats, never boots. He doesn't eat sandwiches, and he won't shovel snow. He can go wherever he wants. He's a free man, is he not? A resident in a land of liberty.

Her mother twists and squirms by his side. She's losing her leverage. Nothing left to use on him, no reason to make him stay. "When?" she demands. "When are you going?"

"Whenever I feel like it."

With that, he's off to the door at a jaunty walk. Out to

slip and slide down the wintry driveway in his flat-soled shoes. Off to make people better. Away to save lives.

And yet, he always comes back in the evenings. He returns to them with the same ho-hum allegiance he has to certain cities, certain hotels. Is it her mother's cooking? The thick, soft towels? The wallpaper? His women – all of them – will never stop wondering why he goes home to his wife.

For her mother, he's like a steep, greased concrete cone. No use trying to climb on top. She'll have to endure these midlife antics. She'll have to wait for him to crumble. Her mother is confident in eventualities. But not too confident. Right now she plots. Devises ways to bamboozle his fun. She'll ship Sal along as his de facto chaperone. She's already making a list, packing the bags in her mind.

Bon voyage.

When Sal and her father get home with their dirty tans and their dirty laundry, everything will be the same. The same, but more complicated, layered, lacquered in place. Her mother will regale them with announcements. How grand it was to have peace and quiet. No dishes, no clutter, no cast-off clothing. God bless solitude! How delightful to be alone.

LADIES IN WAITING

The hotel is a whitewashed place with trellises and colonnades. He has one room. Sal's adjoins his. There are shuttered windows and ceiling fans. Everything is white or wicker. "Where is everyone?" he grumbles from the moment they arrive. There are no children here to speak of. No swing sets, no bicycles for rent.

Mostly she swims in the ocean. When her eyes get tired of the brine, there is the swimming pool. A vast white rectangle with no one in it. At each corner there is a gargoyle or a marble boy peeing into the water. A giant flight of steps rises out of the shallow end. A fountain cascades down the middle. The steps go all the way up the hillside. She can see the wide, swaying leaves in the garden at the very top.

At first her father goes with her. He flaps a newspaper in a deck chair. When she gets bored, he has to coax to get her out. She swims to the middle and pretends not to hear him. She plunges underwater. He leaves. There is no lifeguard, but it doesn't occur to him to worry about her drowning. Like many people of his age and nationality, he can't swim. He does a brave, crippled head-out crawl, slapping the water with his fingers spread wide. People get tired just watching him. Sal, on the other hand, can sink, float and hold her breath for a minute or more. It's as if she were born in the water. He thinks she's better off than he is. Better off, perhaps, without him. Other parents don't do this. *Be careful,* they say. *Look out!* They concern themselves with the world's hazards, with every little thing.

The whole time they are there in Martinique, the clouds part at night and coagulate in the morning. If it's not raining it's overcast, the air soupy with heat. Her father says her mother would be pleased.

They eat breakfast outside at a round table overlooking a

courtyard of drooping hibiscus flowers. Frangipani, bougain-
villea, poinsettia. Everywhere she looks there are big obscene
blossoms. Each morning they choose a different table depend-
ing on where the other diners are – old people, couples – but
every day they sit in the same formation, she at six o'clock,
he at twelve. He doesn't hug or touch her. Not anymore. She
has begun to make him uncomfortable. It has to do with
growing.

The wait staff is black. Not just dark brown but black like
the skins of old forgotten bananas. Her father likes to boss
them around. They wear white cotton shirts with mandarin
collars. White gloves. Their feet don't make a sound. They
carry out pots of jelly and marmalade on silver trays. She
points to the flavour she wants, and they drop a dollop onto
her toast. Some of them, the busboys, are teenaged boys.
They have shiny black eyes and long eyelashes. They come
out from the kitchen smothering their smiles, as if they've
just been horsing around.

Sal lies against a hump of pillows, a tempest in her guts. A
book titled *Camille* rests in her lap. Her eyes travel over and
over the lines. It stops her from worrying about vomiting,
which is worse than the experience itself.

The door between their rooms is ajar. In the bathroom
he trims his moustache and shaves his neck. He clips his
nose hairs with a pair of nail scissors.

There's a knock at the door. Her father answers it. It's a
woman on staff who takes care of the guests after hours. A
short woman with a big round bum and an English accent.

She wears a short-sleeved suit and a name tag that reads *Marlena*. She sinks down onto the edge of the bed and feels Sal's cheek with the back of her hand. "Poor thing," she says. "It's probably just the heat." Sal's father nods along with her lay diagnosis without mentioning a doctorly word. He's called her here for the mothering. Sympathy is women's work. "I'll bring you some mineral water," says Marlena, rubbing Sal's arm. She stands and tugs her skirt down.

Where are you going, Marlena? Sal wants to lay her head down in a lap.

"You swallowed seawater. And you're dehydrated." Her father says this as if it's all her fault. "Drink lots of water. A little bit at a time." He performs appendectomies and installs pacemakers. He does laparoscopy. But as a father he's farcical. He stinks of aftershave. His clothes make her eyes hurt. He sports an almond-coloured suit and a maroon silk shirt with the buttons undone down his breastbone. A fuchsia silk handkerchief in the pocket.

"Can I have some money?" she asks.

"What for?" He is roaming the rooms. He is searching his pockets. He is venturing out on the prowl. "You're not going anywhere."

"What if I have an emergency?" she asks.

He makes exasperated sounds in his throat and flips open his wallet. "You are spoiled." An American fifty-dollar bill flutters down onto her bedcovers. "Who will marry a spoiled girl like you?"

The pimp-dad strikes out into the night.

A resort with no women! – his whole life is an underdog bet, about the impossible score. Which one of the staff will he try? There is the cocktail waitress, who is twenty-two. She is saving her money for school. Or the mulatto singer who trills on the stairs . . . In the future, her mother will say that he's locked in his genetics, his bodily drives. He will claim that he's trapped in his mind, invisible to himself, always in danger of disintegrating. The women are interchangeable. All he has to do is buy them drinks. All they have to do is call him by name.

Once he's gone Sal watches an elephant birth on TV. Where is Marlena? Why won't she bring her some water?

Later, much later, he stumbles back alone in the dark and strews clothes all over the floor. In the morning Sal spies him through the gap between the door hinges. He bumps the corner with his shoulder and staggers naked to the bathroom. His flat brown bum. The lardy fat at his hips. He stands at the toilet, and his narrow back flutters.

THE EDGE OF THE WORLD

The sand on the beach looks like sugar. The palm grove grows denser and denser away from the water. Beyond the palms, a high wall surrounds the resort. A path through the brush winds all the way around the perimeter. Here she finds crabgrass, shoeless footprints in the dirt. Beer bottles, plastic bags, a short green snake.

A boy.

She comes upon him trying to open a coconut by dashing it on the ground.

"That won't work," she informs him. He picks up the coconut and launches it again.

A man comes towards them out of the bush. A man in shorts with big black knobs for knees. A machete dangles from his hand. He lays it in the sand. The blade is tarnished and rusty.

"You don't want that one," he says. "It's been in floating in the sea." He goes deep into the palms and comes back with two green coconuts, which he hacks apart in a few deft strokes. The man peels back the hard shells, revealing moist coconut fur. He cuts spouts, hands one to the boy, the other to Sal. Instead of saying thank you, she stares at his bare flat feet, his spreading toes.

"My daughter has a birthday," he says, "she get an apple. If she peel it all in one piece, she get a new dress." He wipes his knife on his shorts. "If not, she get an apple." Then he goes away.

The boy's mother descends upon them from out of nowhere. She has fascinating red fingernails and a black straw hat with a wide, wide brim. She shakes the boy's shoulder and scolds him in French. She confiscates the coconut, then turns to Sal and snaps, "I am telling him not to take things from strangers." This woman wears a white swimsuit and a red sarong. How can this woman know, just by looking, to speak English, not French?

THEY ARE WHO THEY ARE
(AND WHAT THAT MAKES YOU)

Sal wears a white eyelet sundress to dinner. "You look like a tart," says her father. It was a present from her mother, who bought it in Playa del Carmen. "Why don't you throw that away?" Sal shrugs, as usual, and ignores him. Tonight he wears a merely modestly grotesque ensemble, a teal short-sleeved shirt with a cravat.

When the French woman and her French son arrive at their table, her father forgets all about the sundress and Sal's mother and last year's vacation to Mexico. The woman holds a purse that looks like a sleek black envelope. She wears a black tube dress and delicate gold chains that hang at her neck in three symmetrical loops. He sets his knife and fork down. She asks if they may join them. Her father struggles with a chair for the woman, who introduces herself as Lisette. Her son's name is Tan.

She and Tan are from Montreal. Her father beams. He is also Canadian, and now there is more to talk about. When the waiter comes back, Sal's father makes a scene. The fish is not fresh. The wine is warm. The staff dives into a tizzy of doting and checking and pouring.

Lisette is a stewardess. She has been all over the world, with Tan and without. Her family is Moroccan and Jewish. Sal's father has parents who live in a backward Third World country. They still eat with their fingers. But he will always eat like a surgeon, taking careful stabs with his fork and knifing things apart.

A burst of sun appears on the horizon. Sal's father whacks her on the back of the head for her rhythmic kicking of the table leg. He reaches and captures a wedge of Sal's chicken on the tines of his fork. Sal glares at him in both a private and public way. He smiles triumphantly behind his eyes, puts her food in his mouth and chews.

Tan fashions an animal mouth from a melon rind and jaws it towards her plate.

"Can I go?" Sal whines. Her father looks at Lisette and shrugs.

Lisette says something to Tan in French. He gets up from his chair.

But there's nothing to do. Tan doesn't speak English, and the resort has been fully explored. They wander down to the beach and throw stones at palm trunks. Tan cuts lines in the sand with his heel. They take turns throwing from greater and greater distances. She misses and misses. Tan nails the trunk every time. It makes a hollow thwack, like an enormous wooden drum. The twilight casts a strange pall on the sand. She can see only the white of Tan's teeth and eyes. The game is boring, as games are when you're no good at them.

Eventually she returns to her room. Her father's is empty. Sal opens the window and crawls into bed. The air is fragrant. The sky, sugared with stars.

Her father's key rasps into the lock. He sails in and collapses onto his bed. "Moroccan and a Jew!" he says in wonderment, as if there is an amazing paradox to this fact, to Lisette. What's so special? Lisette's parents are Moroccan

Jews. She lives in Montreal and works as an Air Canada stewardess. Hardly the same thing at all.

A HOLLOW ORGAN, FOUR VESICLES THAT SQUEEZE THE BLOOD AROUND IN THE BODY

At home, her father's distaste for her mother can barely be concealed. He prepares for himself the one dish he knows: cheese on toast. He dirties five knives, creates a profusion of crumbs for her to sweep with her sorrowful rags. These days he sneers at everything she does. She walks into a room and melts at the sight of him. She loses track of herself and flings her arms around his neck. The more he tries to paw her away, the tighter she clings. In the coming months, she will find him increasingly scarce. He's going to pack up his bags and flee for days at a time.

Now there are fights.

Now Sal goes to public school. Her mother prefers it that way – she's saving, bracing for something.

In science class the teacher brings in the heart of a deer he has hunted and shot. It is wrapped in newspaper like a roast from the butcher. He shows the aorta, the vena cava, the pulmonary artery – severed vessels that look a lot like calamari. The class is in awe of this gore. They crowd the desk while he probes the heart's chambers with the cap of a Bic pen.

This is also what her father does for a living. He gets inside people. He pokes around in their guts.

Her parents don't discuss his philandering. They're well beyond it and deep into something else. Her mother walks into a room and asks him, "You hate me, don't you? Because I'm old and fat."

"Yes," he says without looking directly at her. "I hate you. It's because you're old and fat."

Her mother seethes inside. She lays down curse upon silent curse.

MARXISM & FEMINISM

When Sal is nearly a woman, her mother starts to warn her about males as if they aren't human beings at all but snuffling, bad-mannered wildlife, which, for the most part, they are. She dates varsity players, frat boys from the house down the road. Not dates, exactly, because there are no dinners with the parents, no restaurants, no engagements besides sex in cars and in back yards at night.

These are rough approximations of love. Her boyfriends fumble with her zippers and hooks. They smear her breasts against her ribs. They like to leave her genitals throbbing as if soreness measures the good job they have done. They are boys who need to get the ball between the goalposts, the puck into the net. But she picks them out of crowds, the muscles and the numbered jerseys. She picks them from a hundred yards away, these oafish, hard-partying types, because their desires are simple and unequivocal. In later life these boys will make excellent canned ham salesmen, aficionados of porn. They will never be surgeons. They have nothing to give and nothing to take away.

She, on the other hand, will go away to a university on the opposite ocean. Her father is going to pay for it. She'll cash her father's cheques while developing a catalogue of reasons not to go home. She will think of his money as compensation. The whole world owes her something.

Her parents will settle into an uncomfortable détente, related by her mother during long-distance chat. They'll sleep in separate bedrooms. It's a paradox: everyone will get along swimmingly, and they've never been farther apart. Her parents will move. Her parents, who could never see the difference between the U.S. and Canada, are going to buy a row house in Boston. In the week after her parents sell her childhood home, Sal will dream of thieves who come to ransack and loot it.

Sal acquires her first real boyfriend. He stays with her for a year. On his way out, he says she is cold as winter. She thinks of herself as flat, a white-hard drift of snow. Her classes are tripe. People suck. Life bores her to death and back. Her father starts his new job with the bigger salary and more respect for his authority. Sal reads Adorno and *écriture féminine*. She does menstrual upkeep by the light of the moon. Her father buys a new car. Sal calls him a rich pig on the phone. He hangs up. She calls his secretary and pretends to be his lover. But the cheques inscribed with his flouncy signature continue to sail through her mail slot.

ONE OF THOSE CRISP, SEMI-CLOUDY DAYS IN NEW ENGLAND WHEN THE LIGHT IS INSIPID AND NO ONE KNOWS WHAT CLOTHES TO PUT ON IN THE MORNING

In the short little stretch of driveway between the new car and the new house, this is what her father will wear: A dashing shirt constructed of mesh. A visor. Pastel golfing trousers the shade of spumoni. He will have a velvet blazer slung over an arm, his briefcase in hand. Espadrilles on his feet.

The neighbour, who walks stiffly and religiously to his work as an accountant, will look out over his square of lawn and fixate on these clothes, thinking them faggy and ridiculous and more than a little bit threatening. A saucy breeze will stir up. The neighbour will lift his hand in a noodly way. The wave won't be noticed. Sal's father will look down at the hopscotch of driveway where his feet weave along. Where they stutter and trip down the asphalt. The neighbour will balk at this apparent drunkenness. The turning leaves will flutter and shimmy. The neighbour will stare at the shoes, his mind archiving the exact garish shade of the canvas. For a long time after he will see that colour behind his eyes as the colour of guilt.

Sal's father will topple, land with his arms at his sides as if his brain has gone on strike somewhere between vertical and horizontal planes. It won't be pretty. He will have bashed his head on the lamppost. He will have vomited. Blood will leak from his black hair onto the black pavement so that the paramedic has to touch it to confirm what it is. It will come up on her latexed fingers, red, a surprise to everyone but her. He'll be *conveyed*, not rushed, back to the hospital he came from.

Sal's mother, *far too late*, as if she has driven the most circuitous route there, as if she has climbed the stairs instead of taking the elevator, will run howling down the hall, her skirt flapping, her coat undone, her purse dangling by one strap, her hair fallen theatrically from its arrangement, everything come undone. She'll collide with a doctor, a doctor she knows. It's her husband's colleague, a recent family friend.

This stranger, not her mother, will call Sal in another country, on the other side of the continent. It will be six o'clock in her time zone when she answers the phone. She will be wearing her coat. She'll be on her way out to a movie she doesn't want to see with a date she already dislikes. The first thought through her mind will be this: *Now I have a good excuse to stay home.*

The doctor will talk like a professional who knows it's best to spill out bad news in a single pour. Something will have grown and metastasized and squeezed the vessels behind her father's eyes, causing headaches, dizziness and – the rest is the rest. What will Sal call these intracranial fireworks? They will come with a medical term attached, but whatever it is, Sal will forget it the second she hears its name.

There will be a funeral. She'll forget about that, too, the time and the place, like a date with a dentist who wants to drill into her nerves.

GETTING AWAY WITH IT

The house goes on the market but it just won't move. The house comes off the market until spring when the prospects are supposedly better. Her mother complains she's stranded in Massachusetts, penned into a towering house with a room and a half on each floor. She spends a lot of time dealing with his financial advisers, insurance agents and lawyers. She says they are fleecing her with their fees and percentages. Death and money don't go so well together. She blames it all on America.

Sal flies resentfully to Boston for Christmas. There is snow on the roads. People clip around the sidewalks wearing their cold-weather faces. Where are the cedar trees? Where are the neighbourhood dogs?

Her mother's house is immaculate. There is a plastic tree in the living room and a Presto log in the fireplace, and her mother is in the middle of it all, looking bugged-out and strange. As if to explain her demeanour, she says she's been visiting a psychiatrist. Of course a shrink and not an analyst. An analyst would treat her psyche like a layered thing, fossilized and compressed. He would dig it out and dust it off without breaking or missing any of the pieces. But that's not what her mother wants. She is going to do this archaeological procedure in reverse. She is going to bury her husband with Paxil.

Sal has inherited a lot of money. She can have it when she's thirty, if she's a good girl and achieves the miraculous success expected of her. How, when she's so tired? Her eyelids droop by lunchtime. She wanders around the hot and fretful house like a zombie, afraid to go out into the city. If she fell asleep on the train she could wind up in Connecticut. Ironically, the thing that makes her feel sluggish and apathetic during the day keeps her awake at night staring at the ceiling. What is this thing? It eludes words. It even slips from her mind, like a liquid, like oil.

"Maybe you should see someone, too," her mother suggests.

Sal is not so sure. Where did this idea come from, that it's good to uncover everything, to analyze and self-reflect, as if she could grasp the *everything* about herself? Repression must have a protective purpose. All this run-of-the-mill crisis is supposed to make them tougher and at the same time more resilient. It is supposed to make them deeper, more compassionate human beings. Well, fuck that. They are not better people. They sulk about and bitch at one another. They try to kill each other with belligerence.

Death, compared to the people they are now, is harmless and neutral. It's not the loss or the grieving either. It's all the black crud of memory, the stuff of their family triangle, that they're afraid of. And it gets worse than that. It's the deep, ugly, unmentionable sediment at the bottom of their thoughts, the worst of it being this: they couldn't *wait* for him to die. On more than one occasion, at the lowest point of the curve, they even *joked about doing him in.*

Couldn't wait to get their hands on his money.

Couldn't wait to get him out of their lives.

Talking cure? She'd rather hold her own guts in her hand.

This is how they will get through. Her mother will do it with pharmaceuticals, a cocktail of mood elevators and sedatives. Sal will become a swollen oilfield, a gusher waiting to happen. She will go out and fuck all the self-destructive, sex-addicted losers in the world. She is going to get high on the drama of pointless romance. Bring on the narcissists. Bring on the assholes. She is going to let them dig into her. She is going to light the geyser on fire.

And yet. Her mother arrives at her bedside at 4 a.m. She suddenly wants to know all about the other women. About every single one.

"He didn't love any of them," says Sal. "Go back to bed."

"It's easier to tell the truth," her mother says in reply.

"No, it isn't." Is it not, in fact, better to get wrapped up in fictions? A little lie lubricates the unpleasant facts. A little lie gets them closer and at the same time takes them away.

EVERYONE MUST SAY
THEY DO SOMETHING

On a plane from Montreal to Vancouver Sal witnesses a prairie brushfire. It looks like nothing from above, a black circle the size of a quarter with a hem of smoke billowing at its fringes. The sky, at cruising altitude, is not really blue but a vanishing white-blue. Her gaze gets lost in the depth and texture of things. Her mind in strata of clouds.

Everyone must work. Everyone must say they do something. So since university, ten years ago, Sal has worked. Now she toils for an import-export company, motivated by inter-mittent ambition. She trades in bamboo and rattan, tables made out of endangered hardwood. She skips all over South-east Asia. Bali. Sumatra. Bangkok. Saigon. She buys and sells. She knows where to look for shoddy design. But under-neath this routine, she senses another verb tugging at the corners of her life. A word – to do with *looking*, not *getting*, obscured in busyness and flight.

Montreal. A city that's never as quaint and cosmopolitan as the idea in her head. She leaves it feeling queasy, light-headed and free.

Sal waits at the baggage carousel. Suitcases are picked off the ratcheting plates. Passengers are kissed and embraced by their welcoming parties. They depart until there's nothing left to tumble out from between the rubber flaps. Sal won-ders drearily what's become of her bag. She looks up. Next to her a tall woman with sleek blonde hair drops her toe on the floor again and again. She looks like Miss Sweden. Dangling from her finger is a plastic boutique bag the size of a Pop-Tart. She drinks a drink through a straw. The woman calls out over the carousel. "Tan!" Her voice is startling and pow-erful. The name is her husband's, Sal can tell from her tone – someone who needs reminding, who's always in danger of wandering away.

Sal's body grows hot. Patches begin to sweat from the floor up. Her arches, armpits, the back of her neck. Sal picks at faces in the dwindling crowd. Who is she looking for? She doesn't even know.

A man arrives from behind and inserts himself into the space between Sal and the tall blonde. His wife asks, "What did they say?"

"I gave them our claim stubs." His accent is arrestingly Québécois.

An article of their baggage, it seems, has also gone astray. But what does it matter? It's his wife with the sharp, expensive tastes. The boots with heels that could split furniture apart. This is a man who doesn't give a shit about clothes. He is dressed like a well-paid social worker, a borderline nerd. He is the kind of guy who has dandruff, who sloughs himself continually. Not, in fact, handsome in the least.

Miss Sweden crosses the room to throw her drink in the garbage. Her heels tap heavily, confidently across the floor. Stupidly, without a single thought about consequences, Sal taps this man on the shoulder. He bends to the bag on the floor by his feet. Sal's reach is exaggerated, a stretch.

"Do I know you?" Sal asks as he comes back up with the leather handle in his grip. Tan straightens his shoulders and looks at Sal. His facial muscles twitch. Blood pulses through Sal's capillaries. Each pore is a sweltering pinpoint. He is flipping back the cards in his mind, parsing the possibilities.

"No," he says. "No." She sees he has cut himself shaving. She sees that he is lying.

"Your mother's name is Lisette," says Sal.

He turns his head ten mistrustful degrees to the left. His right eye's gaze meets Sal's right eye. *Don't*, it warns.

His wife returns. Her eyes dart between them. She is doing the algebra, solving for the unknown variable, deciding that Sal is not quite tall or beautiful or dangerous enough.

There's a flutter through the upper lengths of her intestines. They stand around uncomfortably like three sides of a lopsided triangle.

"Okay," Sal says meanly. She lifts her shoulders into a shrug. "Well, I was wrong." Well, dying. Melting into the floor.

Now they are smiling weirdly and sidling away. They are shedding her. He guides his wife with two fingers and a thumb at the small of her back. *Wait just a fucking minute.* Sal's gaze burns into the tripod of fingers, the hand's width of his wife's coat. Sal is not finished here. Sal is never finished with anything.

But they are. They breeze off towards the doors. Towards a taxi and wherever the hell it is they sleep at night.

SO THIS IS HOW IT WILL BE

Sal lives in a two-bedroom condo – purchased with inheritance – in a building full of soundproof artist's lofts, though she's no artist and neither are any of her neighbours. The second bedroom is a space she doesn't know how to fill. It's a room with a sewing table and a sofa bed where friends sleep when they get too drunk to drive. Her room is simple and white with a high wooden bed where she's woken in the middle of the night by the phone.

It's Tan.

"How did you get my number?" she asks, shooting up-right from the mattress.

"I remembered your last name."

"Do you live here? Or there?" Will she have to fly to Montreal for the rest of her life?

"Here," he says.

She sighs with a kind of relief. "Come over," she says.

"Now?" He's whispering. His wife must be asleep.

"Tomorrow."

So. They are going to sneak around like lovers.

A DISEASE OF FORGETTING

Tan arrives at her door with light-years under his arm, with time both stretched and compressed – since they spoke on the phone, since they met in the Caribbean, since they were ten, since her last contact with another human, mere hours ago on the way home from work. She talked to the cashier at the liquor store where she stopped to buy two bottles of wine. She thought they were going to need alcohol.

He steps into her apartment, zooming out of Sal's imagi-nation and crashing right into the unremarkable now. He moves reluctantly into the kitchen, where he sits awkwardly in his coat until she coaxes it out from under him. On the way to the closet she sniffs the lining. Dog and shampoo. She pokes a hanger into the shoulders, shoves her coats aside to make room.

When she returns he's scowling at the wall. Sal sits down. He has picked up a catalogue off the table. He flips it by the spine. Who is this man at her kitchen table, gone from dark blond to grey? She's missed some prime phases, some pupal steps. She looks at him physically for traces of his mother, but there are none. He's only himself.

He is testy. He doesn't like her wine.

Tan says he's a civil engineer. He lives in a house he designed himself. From the sky it's the shape of a cloverleaf. His wife is a member of Mensa. His child, a musical prodigy.

Where Tan maximizes, Sal minimizes. She goes under, not over. She's a sales manager who can't do math. She has a rotation of part-time boyfriends, each oblivious to the other. What she has is a leather couch.

"My mother lives in Paris with her husband," Tan announces. Her *third* husband. He says this like it's somebody's fault. Maybe Sal's.

Well, she tells him, her father is dead. She says this with weighty respect as people do when discussing the departed. So-and-so *passed on.* And truly her father has done so. Like a stranger on a platform as the train whizzes by.

He was so very smart. He died of a mental implosion. But here's what he did best: he vanished. On the way out, he even swept himself from her memory.

Sometimes Tan comes over. Sometimes he doesn't. They go out to restaurants and tie up the tables. *Go away,* they growl at the waiters. *Leave us alone.* They go to the movies and talk their way through to the credits. People in adjacent seats have to tell them to shut up.

On the fifth night of their Caribbean vacation or perhaps it was the sixth – who cares what night it was? They are probably making it up – her father did not return to his room. Neither did Tan's mother. Where did they go?

Their parents' affair lasted eight years. They ran away from their lives, pretending to be husband and wife. They played golf. They strolled. They took other vacations, with Tan and without.

So what.

Sal examines Tan's forearms – the light olive skin, the veins wiggling under the surface – and she thinks about biting him. It's because he wants to rearrange her furniture. To slap her with his facts. She thinks she'd like to fuck him. Make a mark for someone to find. She wonders if they will *ever* be lovers. She could devour him like food or suck him up through her nose. Does heroin feel this way? Does love?

MIGHTY CONTESTS

They are slumming it at an equidistant point between their residences. They are drinking coffee at 10 p.m. out of cardboard cups. They are scraping their chairs in and resting their elbows on a table the width of a clock face at a place where you can get crullers and black-market cigarettes at any time of the day or night. They are sitting down with their coats on.

Tan drops his *petite histoire* as if he's been saving it up. In Martinique, his mother's gaze found some earrings in a shop window. She stepped inside and watched the proprietor cut facets into emeralds. Sal's father went back later and bought them. "He fell in love with my mother," Tan says in a haughty tone. "He gave her the earrings like a prize for a contest she'd won." He sits back, folds his arms with a certain smug satisfaction. Then he adds, "She wouldn't take them. They came too easily."

Sal bites the inside of her cheek. "He wanted more than a mistress." She looks past him at a young woman surrounded by textbooks piled open on top of one another like splayed birds. "More than she could ever give."

Tan counters, "Every other weekend he chased her down in the cities along her flight path."

"No, he didn't."

"Yes, he did."

"He fell in love with an *idea*," Sal says, her voice piping, climbing. The girl with the books glances up. "She was a mother who didn't act like one. She was paradoxical. A Moroccan and a Jew."

"She still *is*," Tan corrects.

"She lived in Montreal," says Sal. "She wore hats and elegance like someone who was born there." Sal's father tried to chase her down along with everything else he'd been trying to buy. A cure for intractable loneliness. An antidote to the big, bad world.

"He sent her horribly written letters. She didn't answer one of them."

"She didn't write letters!" Sal hisses. "She phoned in the middle of the night and hung up on my mother!"

"He flew to Montreal and drove a rental car to our house in the suburbs! He couldn't find it and called from a pay phone! She told him to go to hell!"

"He couldn't speak French!" Sal shutters her face with her hands. "He couldn't read the signs."

"All right," he says in a softer tone. He starts to rub tiny incompetent circles into Sal's back. "All right." He thinks he's made her cry. Sal knows he thinks weeping is a freaky feminine phenomenon. He has a wife and a daughter. He's the kind of guy who'll have only daughters and never figure out how to handle them.

Sal wipes her hands down her face. "I'm going home," she says. They have worn each other out.

"But it's only eight o'clock." He looks haggard behind the eyes.

In a week, he comes over without invitation. She blocks the doorway with her body. He lays his hand on her arm. She gazes down at the fingernails trimmed square, the hairs on the backs of his fingers.

"You were right," he says. "That's not how it went at all."

Their parents' affair ended, as mostly they do, messily and inevitably. "After that she married the first jerk she could find." Husband Number Two moved in. Tan moved out. Unwittingly into a house full of junkies. He was sixteen. His grandmother visited him and cried. "My mother was in love with love," he says bitterly. "She was a stupid romantic flake."

They are still in the hallway. They step inside and close the door.

"What about your dad?" Sal whispers. "Where the hell was he?"

He studies the ceiling. His eyes are glistening.

Light-years before, they met on a Caribbean island. They bashed open coconuts, and they lost all the milk. They hurled stones at palm trees, angry even then.

LOTUSES

A mental revolution. Sal's mother reads a book about the Aral Sea. She drops the book on the floor. Then joins a group of environmental crusaders. At the library she blazes through books and more books, reinventing herself as unofficial expert on hydrology and watersheds. Now she says things like, *Snow is water in the bank.* Forget history. Now she's got dogma, schisms, politics. Depression gives way to radical slants, bouts of proactivity.

"I'm moving," her mother tells Sal on the phone.

"But why?"

"Because now I can."

Miami. The lower-opposite corner of the continent. By herself to live in a condo. Miami, to hang with the pink flamingos and the drug lords. Families are supposed to get bigger, knit closer. Sal's is a shrinking deconstruction. They haven't made enough of an effort, she and her mother, to stay together. They have talked too much on the phone and not enough in person. Now the distance is doubling.

AN ISLAND OF SWINE

Where is Tan? Three weeks and Sal has heard nothing.

Tan. Sal looks it up. An uncommon name of uncertain origin. Scandinavian or Dutch? It's impossible to tell.

Plus, Sal discovers in her research, dozens of Islands of Flowers: Guernsey, Taboga . . . And an experimental film of the same name about a garbage dump and pigs and rotten tomatoes. Who cares about this irony? What are names beyond words that sound good to certain originators, marketeers and parents?

She calls. Three rings and a hang-up. Then she gets into bed. Right now he could be driving around the city looking for a donair joint that's open. Brushing his teeth at the kitchen sink while his wife monopolizes the bathroom.

Is that the last they will see of each other? The thought makes Sal itch with craziness. She gets out of bed, wanders into the living room and stands there in her underwear. The room is freezing cold. Her skin, on fire. She dials his number and lets it ring to the end. Then she shouts into his voice-mailbox, "What's the point of having a fucking cell phone if you're not going to turn it on?"

She stares into the daisy of perforations in the mouthpiece, listening to the dial tone. After a while it sounds like a choir humming just outside her door. Who does she think she'll call next, his wife? Sal bets his wife, member of Mensa, doesn't give up her shit for the imagination. Or fudge the truth with similes. Or dwell on a man's vapours. Sal is behaving like an actress – as her father would say, *like a woman*. But *this* – a miasma of obsessive thoughts – isn't *like* anything she's tasted or seen or done before. This is a bad habit. She's got to quit it like people quit smoking and fetishes.

Sal lies down flat as people do when they have heart attacks. She rests her cheek on the floor and embraces its solidity. The most solid thing in the world, and it's hers, mortgage-free. This is a telephone. This is a hardwood floor. Nothing is more than it is. Tan has crooked bottom teeth with plaque in between. A blackhead in the coil of his ear.

THE RULE OF TAN

As soon as she turns her back, as soon as she's nearly forgotten, Sal pounces on the phone and the sound of his voice. "Where are you?"

"Double parked," says Tan. "Downstairs."

"I'm not decent," Sal gasps. "Drive around the block." Then she hangs up. The call has left her breathless. Even her hair tingles.

Tan arrives in a filthy, grumbling mood. He kicks his shoes off at the door, staggers in and collapses into an armchair. Sal moons over him with an empty glass in her hand.

"Where have you been?" Why is he back? She wants all of the answers and more. More romance. *Did she love him? How did she love him?* If they must come to their close, she wants a happy, joyous, deep, cathartic release. It doesn't even have to be real.

But Tan is bored, exasperated even, by his own memory. He's concerned with the present tense, with his wife, who is on to them, who is jittery with vigilance and suspicion.

"What do you tell her?" Sal asks.

"My wife? I don't tell her anything."

"Then tell *me* something."

He stands up as if he came just for the satisfaction of leaving. She sets the glass down and dashes to insert herself in his way.

"He bought her an ounce of the most expensive perfume in the world," Tan says cheerlessly. "It came in a little marble bottle shaped like a heart."

"Then?"

"She spilled it in the sink and for months the bathroom smelled like Joy."

Sal wears a kimono, a gift from her mother, who is moving to Florida, a slippery white thing with embroidered flowers and a wine stain on the collar. It slides off her shoulders, which she knows are very nice. "We're friends," she says.

She approaches him gingerly. She reaches for his shirt collar. He bats her hands away.

Tan wears a plastic Timex watch with a Velcro strap. A blue checked shirt that looks like a dishtowel. He shoves the top three buttons through their holes. He pulls his shirttails out from the waist of his unironed pants. When the fabric comes over his head, Sal is surprised by the hair. The nap of it bristling down on his forearms, the triangular shag at his sternum. He flicks the shirt away from his wrists. A tall, broad man with sloping shoulders and a hidden collection of flab at his waist. Everything about him is shifting, sliding downward.

Tan has always been talented at throwing things. Sal can say such things. Tan had good aim when they were children with rocks. He picks her kimono off the floor, wads it into a mound, then hurls it at the wall. It clips a framed photo of Sal in a bobby's hat. It swings on its wire, then comes to rest on a tilt.

"We aren't friends," he says. His face is a furious, mottled red.

Next he wrestles her camisole over her head. She bought it at a pink lingerie store in Singapore. It used to be white, but now it's ivory from too many trips through the wash. Sal lifts her arms like a girl put to bed without supper. More roughly still, her pyjama bottoms fastened at the waistband with a safety pin. The pin pops open and scrapes an inch of her belly. After that, there's nothing else. Her good underwear is all in the laundry.

"The most expensive perfume in the world," he sneers. "Do you like that?"

Her eyes pan around the room and out the window.

"Look at me," he says. "I made it up."

In the apartment across the street, in the mercurial glow of a TV, someone pedals an exercise bike. Someone else folds towels.

pushes her backwards over the arm of the couch. She lands on her back in the cushions. He plucks his shirt off the floor and whips it once as if to snap out the wrinkles. "Guess what? My mother's name is Pascale, not Lisette." A mist of angry spit showers over her thighs. "She was a famous chemist. So was my father. Together they won the Nobel Prize." Sal slides her legs away from him, creeps backwards down to the far end of the sofa.

"Don't shut your eyes. My name isn't Tan. I never lived with junkies. I went to boarding school and then to the Sorbonne." He thrusts his arms back into the sleeves of his shirt, mismatches the buttons and holes.

He turns. Sal glares at his hunched back, listens to him stomp out through the rooms of her apartment. "I'm a fucking millionaire!" he shouts. His shoes land, one, then the other, on the tiles in the hall. Coat hangers jangle.

Her front door slams open but not shut. Sal flies from the couch, retrieves her kimono, does a sloppy job of parcelling her nakedness. She muddles out of the apartment and into the hall where a corner of his brown coat flashes away. "Liar!" she calls out after him. But it's no good – the elevator doors are closing.

Closing. It's not how this – how anything – should end, with a glimpse of coat that's the colour of a rodent. "Liar!" she calls. She's half dressed and barefoot, and even now her lava is cooling. The illuminated numbers descend. Where is Tragedy when you need it? With a clunk at the bottom of the shaft and a sigh of hydraulic air, it rages down and forward and on.